How Green You Are!

Each of the chapters in *How Green You Are* is a story in itself – but they all have to do with one lively lot of kids, who all live in the same street. Bee's best friends are Kevin and Julie, but Marie is part of the gang too, though she's inclined to be spiteful; and so is Weird George despite his odd behaviour. In some of the stories the gang is all together – at the local fair where they manage to lose Marie's pet monkey, and at the wedding party in their street when the bride and the groom themselves get lost; in other chapters one special person stands out, as when Julie tells her friends about meeting the ghost of a drowned nun at her convent school.

Encounters with relations and neighbours, friends and the odd enemy or two add up to a book that is at the same time moving, funny and very entertaining – and so vivid that you might expect to meet its characters round your own street corner.

Also by Berlie Doherty

Children of Winter
Dear Nobody
Granny was a Buffer Girl
The Making of Fingers Finnigan
Spellhorn
Tough Luck
Tilly Mint Tales
Tilly Mint and the Dodo
White Peak Farm

Requiem
(an adult novel)

BERLIE DOHERTY

How Green You Are!

Illustrated by Elaine McGregor Turney

MAMMOTH

First published in Great Britain 1982
by Methuen Children's Books Ltd
Published 1992 by Mammoth
an imprint of Reed Consumer Books Limited
Michelin House, 81 Fulham Road, London SW3 6RB
and Auckland, Melbourne, Singapore and Toronto

Reprinted 1993

Text copyright © 1982 Berlie Doherty
Illustrations copyright © 1982 Methuen Children's Books

ISBN 0 7497 1047 0

A CIP catalogue record for this title
is available from the British Library

Printed and bound in Great Britain by
BPCC Paperbacks Ltd
Member of BPCC Ltd

Contents

For Janna, Tim and Sally

1. How green you are!

There was a kid in our street called Julie. None of the others could stand her. She went to a different school from us, a convent school, where they had to wear uniform. The first day she went to that school, I remember, we all followed her up the road to the bus stop, laughing at her. She looked daft. She was wearing a green school coat that was too big for her, so that her little pink hands stuck out all chubby from the sleeves, and she was weighed down with all sorts of rubbish – a shiny brown leather satchel, and a shoe bag with a bunch of roses embroidered on it, and a hockey stick. And she had her hair done in pigtails with green ribbons, and a stupid green hat stuck on her head.

She went bright red when she came out of her house and saw us all waiting on the other side of the road for her. She looked as if she wanted to go back in but her mum kissed her goodbye and shut the door flat in her face and went off back to bed. So Julie smiled at us, in a half-proud, half-scared sort of way, that made her look more as if she was going to burst into tears, and marched up the street, pigtails bobbing, and over the main road to the bus-stop, and stood there gazing across at us with

7

blank eyes while the traffic trundled backwards and forwards between us.

I wanted to shout 'Good luck Julie!' to her, but I daren't, in case the others laughed at me too. So I just stood there while they shouted 'Jolly hockey sticks,' across at her, and then Kevin started them off singing 'How green you are, how green you are, how green you are, how green ...', ever so softly, to the tune of 'Auld Lang Syne', till her bus came, and then they sang it at the tops of their voices as she staggered onto the bus and

8

moved down to the back seat. She just sat there, staring out at us with her face all blank and closed up, as if she couldn't see us any more, and as the bus lurched forward we all waved and ran off to our big school up the hill.

But I felt a bit sad about all that. Julie had been my friend, sort of my best friend, up till then. We used to play marbles in the alley-way together, and sail paper boats down the gutter when it rained, and we'd spent all our hot summers together playing rounders on the field over the railway line and helping with the donkey-rides on the beach. It felt as if none of that had ever happened. I trailed up the hill after the others, thinking how different she looked wearing that stiff new uniform instead of her tatty little cotton dress and gym shoes. Marie was waiting for me and when I caught up with her she linked her arm in mine.

'That's her gone, the snob!' she said. 'Will you be my best friend now, Bee?'

She'd been wanting to be my best friend for ages.

And I had to say yes, because I didn't want to be called a snob too.

But I kept thinking about her during the day. It was a new school for us too, but at least we were all there together, and had been in Junior School together. It must have been really strange for her, going to a new school all on her own, and a convent school at that, with nuns like great black crows floating down the corridors and carrying her off to chapel. I was dying to know what it was like. So on my way home from school I bought a bar of Cadbury's, and I dashed to her house after tea, when none of the other kids were around. I thought we'd sit on her step, like we always did, and share out the Cadbury's, and I'd tell her about our school and she'd tell me all about the nuns and everything, but when she opened the door she just stood there, all clean and different in her stiff long uniform still, and said, 'I can't possibly play out tonight. I've got Latin homework to do.'

That did it. I ran off round to Marie's and we shared out the Cadbury's bar, and then we went and played ball against Julie's house.

Marie wasn't as good as Julie, though. She was a rotten catch.

At the weekend there were a bunch of us playing down in the alley-way near Julie's house. There'd been a cowboy film on telly that afternoon and all the little ones had come out in their cowboy hats and were firing caps off at cats and down letter-boxes. Kevin and Marie and I were trying to organise them into tribes and wagon trains so we could do the film when Julie sauntered up.

'Can I play?' she said at last, after we'd ignored her about ten minutes.

I remembered the bit about the Latin homework and gave Marie half of my last stick of bubble-gum. All the kids were watching us.

Then Kevin said, 'I bet you'd like to be an Indian Princess, wouldn't you, Julie?' Her eyes lit up. The star part! We looked at him in disgust and just stood there popping our bubble-gum while he explained to her that she had betrayed her tribe and would have to be tied to the totem-pole.

I suddenly cottoned on to what he was up to, and I

ran and fetched our short washing-line, the one my mum used for dusters and tea-cloths. We tied Julie to the lamp-post with it, wound it round and round, and then the little ones all skipped round her while she did a fantastic Indian chant and vowed eternal loyalty to the tribe of Big Chief Sitting Bull. Then she started going on about her new red tap-shoes, and how the music nun wanted to teach her violin because she had such good pitch, and we all joined up in a long line, each with a

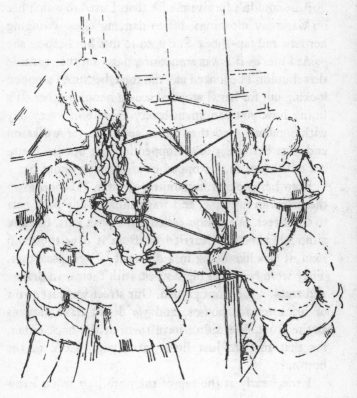

hand stretched out on to the shoulder of the one in front, and we began to march round her, chanting very softly 'How green you are, how green you are, how green you are, how green ...' and then louder and louder as we danced away from her still in our long Indian file, till we got right to the top of our street where we played another game altogether, totally ignoring the yells of fury from the lamp-post, and when our mums called us in to tea we all ran in and forgot about her.

Julie couldn't forgive me for that. I used to watch her on Saturday mornings, off to dancing class, swinging her new red tap-shoes. She used to toss her head as she passed me, as if I was something nasty on the roadside that shouldn't be looked at. And then, because I stopped looking out for her, I stopped seeing her altogether. It's funny how you can spend every minute of every day with someone, and then never see them for weeks on end, just because you'd stopped looking out for them. To tell the truth, I stopped even thinking about her.

I saw her one evening, quite a bit later. I'd been down the prom on my bike, and was riding up the posh part to our street. We always called it the posh part, because although our street carried on from it over the main road, it was like being in a different village altogether. They were beautiful big houses, with their own drives, and trees in the front garden. Our street was just a row of brick terrace houses, and we didn't have gardens at the front. We didn't have them at the back either, for that matter. Just little yards with w.c.'s at the bottom.

I was nearly at the top of the posh part when I saw

Julie getting out of a car. She must have been given a lift home from school with someone's dad, because there were two other girls in the car in green uniforms. She said, in a funny, plummy, prim voice, 'Thank you ever so much for the lift. It was very kind of you,' and shut the car door. Then, instead of running over the main road to our street, she stood waving for a bit and then walked backwards down the posh part and started going up someone's drive. She waited there a bit and then dashed up the road and crossed over to our street. I couldn't believe it. She'd been letting on that she lived in one of those posh houses.

Soon after that I saw her big sister Barbie in Mrs Marriot's. Mrs Marriot was a woman up our street who used to sell things in her front room. It wasn't like a shop, because everything she sold she'd made herself. She'd have things in trays on their table – cakes and bread and ginger biscuits and cough candy – but it was really queer because when you went in you couldn't smell any of the lovely things laid out on the table. All you could smell was boiled fish. They'd three cats. You sometimes got bits of cat fur stuck to your toffee-apple. Mrs Marriot was an old woman with frizzy red hair and no teeth. She was always laughing, and her gums were all pink and wet and shiny. Her husband only had one leg, and he used to sit in the corner all the time and wave his stick at you if he thought you were pinching anything.

I was standing in front of the tray of toffee-apples trying to make out which one was the biggest when Barbie came in with a jug to be filled with ginger-beer.

It was lovely, Mrs Marriot's ginger-beer. All pale and golden and powdery at the bottom.

'Why don't you go round with our Julie any more?' Barbie asked me. I went scarlet. I could feel it. She made me feel really guilty, asking me that. As if it was all my fault. Julie and I had never fallen out before, and Barbie had always been like a big sister to me, too. I liked her. I remember when she took us to the pantomime in town, and we saved up all our sweets for three weeks to give her as a present. We saved them in a big tin, and when we got to the theatre and she opened it up they were all stuck together in a fluffy lump – pear-drops and fruitgums and licorice torpedoes and polo mints, with bits of hair and silver paper and bus tickets sticking out. Barbie said she'd rather have a cigarette anyway and gave them back to us, but we couldn't break any of them off, so we kept passing this lump backwards and forwards, sucking it and grinding little chunks off it, till we got fed up with it and chucked it on the floor. When we were going out of the theatre at the end of the pantomime I saw a little lad crawl under the seat and put it in his pocket.

I didn't know what to say to Barbie about Julie. I decided I didn't want a toffee-apple any more, even though I'd seen one with a great wedge of toffee stuck to the bottom, so I pretended I'd seen Marie passing in front of the window and I ran out and shouted, 'Wait on, Marie, I've an important message for you.' And I ran off home hoping that Barbie wouldn't come out and see that Marie wasn't there at all.

It was Kevin who told me about Julie's accident. His brother Mike used to take Barbie out on his motor-bike. They'd been engaged twice but she kept breaking it off because he couldn't hold a job down. He was working in the parks just now so he was back in, and apparently he'd had to go round and babysit for them the night before.

'Did you hear what happened to Julie Mills yesterday, Bee?' said Kevin, on the way to assembly.

I pretended that I did know, of course, so he didn't say anything else.

'Go on then,' I said, 'tell us.'

'She had to be rushed to hospital. She was knocked down.'

I felt as if a cold grey hand had wiped itself across my face. Kids were pushing past me down the corridor, all shouting and yelling to each other, and Kevin was carried along with them. It was like watching the tide going out. I ran after him and grabbed his arm to stop him. My legs were shaking. I could see that he was nearly bursting with excitement at having something to tell me that I didn't already know.

'What happened, Kevin? You're kidding, aren't you? You're having me on!'

'Honest! Cross me heart and hope to die. She got knocked down near her school. She went missing from class and one of the teachers went after her. When Julie saw her coming she ran off over the road. Straight into a car.'

I felt sick and faint. I didn't dare ask anything else about it. I just kept seeing her, in her pigtails and her funny long uniform coat, flying across the road and slamming into a car. And lying on the ground.

'Come on, you're not supposed to be here, young lady.' It was Mr Murphy, sweeping up all the kids hiding round the cloakrooms. 'Into assembly, this minute!' My feet just about worked, like heavy blobs at the end of bendy pipe-cleaners. I sat through assembly with all the voices and music floating over me, and every time I closed my eyes I saw Julie lying in the road.

I couldn't catch Kevin again. I could see his bright ginger head bobbing about four rows in front, and then his class all went off to the baths, and by the time he was back I was in triple needlework. I kept seeing her slamming into the car, and lying in the road, and then I saw all those black nuns floating round her and lifting her up so that her head lolled back, and I was there, wanting to say I was sorry, and her eyes were open and blank and staring right through me. Perhaps she was dead! And every time I came to that bit I jerked up in my chair and Miss Ross shouted at me. I didn't even know. I had to find out what had happened.

As soon as the bell went at the end of last lesson that morning I raced out of school. Marie yelled after me to wait but I didn't want to talk to her about it so I chucked my sandwich box over to her and told her she could eat them for me. She couldn't believe her luck.

I ran off down the hill to our street and went down the back alley-way to Julie's, so my mum wouldn't see me. I could hardly breathe by the time I got there; my chest felt as if it was bursting and my throat was clenched tight and my legs were quivering again. I leaned against

16

her wall and gasped for air, and my arms and legs felt like lead weights, like when you climb up out of the baths and all the water's draining off you.

I reached round and tapped on the door. I didn't know what I was going to say to Julie's mum. And I stood there, leaning against the wall with my eyes closed while I heard her trudging down the stairs and fiddling with the door knob. And I felt her standing there.

I opened my eyes and turned round to face her. It was Julie! She was standing there in her nightie with a huge plaster across her cheek and her eye swollen and closed up, and her arm in a sling.

I stood on her doorstep and starting hooting with laughter. I think she thought I was crying at first, I think I might have been, but then she started laughing too, with her face all twisted to one side as if she'd been to the dentist, and she kept gasping and saying, 'Ooh, it hurts! Don't make me laugh, it hurts!' Her mum came down the street steaming from the chip shop, and she rushed us inside and got me to make a pot of tea while she shared them all out between the three of us, and we all sat round their fire eating them. That's the best fish and chips I've ever had.

I felt a bit shy, going back to school, and I hovered on their doorstep thinking what to say.

'I like your school uniform, Julie,' I said. 'I think that green suits you.'

And she grinned at me, with her face all lop-sided. I think she believed me.

2. The haunting of Miss Julie

It was a dark misty night in late December. Julie's mum and dad had gone out to a christmas social in their church hall, and Julie had asked me to stay in and babysit with her. We packed her little brothers off to bed as early as possible and built up the fire really high, and turned the light off. The glow from the flames danced on the furniture and across the ceiling, and the little crackles hissed and spat and gurgled as the coals shifted. Julie brought some chestnuts from the kitchen and we pricked them and laid them on a tin plate over the flames. Every now and then one of them would explode, firing hot pieces of sharp shell at us, and we would suck out the mush of baked chestnut before pitching it back into the flames. It was my favourite sort of evening.

A sudden banging at the window made us both jump to our feet, and set the guinea-pigs scurrying round their box in the corner. Julie answered the door reluctantly and in walked Kevin, bringing all the cold of the winter night in with him, and a jug of Mrs Marriot's ginger beer ... He sat himself down in the hearth and started cracking away at the hot chestnuts with his teeth.

'Why don't you make yourself at home?' asked Julie tartly.

'No option,' said Kevin cheerfully. 'It was either here or the pictures, and I've seen that film twice already. Your Barbie's round at our place, talking about wedding dresses. She isn't half boring, your sister! Anyway, our Mike gave me some money to get rid of me for a couple of hours. Eh, it looks right cosy in here, from outside. I've been standing at the window for ages, pulling faces at you two, but you were that busy stuffing yourselves with chestnuts you never even noticed.'

Julie gave a shriek of horror and drew the curtains abruptly across the windows. The flames in the fire flurried for a moment, flattened, and then settled. The long shadows danced again. The three of us sat in silence, like cats on the hearthrug, our hands and faces burning in the heat.

'Julie,' I said. 'You know when you ran away from your school that time...' Julie didn't answer.

'Why did you do it?'

Kevin and I both looked at her expectantly, but she sat staring into the flames as though she hadn't heard me.

'Go on, Julie, tell us,' said Kevin.

'I don't want to talk about it,' she said primly.

'Ah, you always say that! Go on! It must have been important.'

We knew Julie of old. If there was one thing she loved doing, it was telling stories.

'Did you really hate it?' Kevin prompted.

She sighed, and eased herself onto the hearth, with her back resting against the tiled surrounds.

'It's the most beautiful place you've ever seen,' she said softly. 'You know those high walls you can see from the main road? Well, they go back for miles. The grounds are massive. It's all sort of landscaped round the convent house, and then there's the hockey fields and the tennis courts, and then there's ...'

'Yes?'

'Well, then there's the part you're not supposed to go in. There's this little garden, with tall trees all round it, and that's where the nuns are buried. The nuns' burial ground. And behind that there's the glen ... and that's haunted.'

'Did you ever go in there?' asked Kevin.

'I used to go off on my own a lot,' said Julie. 'You know, at first, nobody would talk to me. They used to make fun of my accent and that, because I wasn't posh like them. They used to laugh at me ...'

I felt guilty then, remembering how we had once made fun of her too. I looked at Kevin, but he wouldn't catch my eye.

'Well,' she said, 'they're all right now, since ... but anyway, when I first started there, I used to go off on my own at lunchtimes, wandering round the grounds exploring, and one day I went into this little graveyard and then into the overgrown part. When I came out some girls from my class were waiting for me, and they told me that I wasn't supposed to go into the glen because it was haunted. I told them they were daft, and that I didn't believe in ghosts, but they insisted that it was true. According to the story, many years ago a young girl had entered the convent because her parents

20

wouldn't let her marry the man she was in love with. Two years later he was killed in the war. When she heard this, the young nun wandered off down to the glen and threw herself into the pond there. They found her there the next morning, floating on the top. They buried her there, in the glen, under a willow tree by the pond. They said they couldn't bury her in consecrated ground because she had committed the sin of suicide. And so she wanders round the glen, gathering wild flowers to put on her own grave, and looking for someone to put her soul to rest and bury her among the Sisters of her order.'

'How sad,' I said.

Kevin nearly choked on a chestnut. 'Julie! You don't mean to tell me you believed rubbish like that, do you?'

I dug my elbow sharply into his back.

'Go on Julie,' I said. 'Did you go in there?'

'I had to, didn't I, Bee?' She prodded the coals gently, making small flames spurt. 'I mean, I thought exactly the same as Kevin. It was rubbish. I wasn't going to let those girls get the better of me by believing a story like that. So next lunchtime, I went down past the playing fields to the far end of the grounds. I didn't let on to anyone, and I made sure no-one had seen me. I slipped into the little burial ground and down to the end and through the tall trees into the glen. It was so quiet in there! I couldn't even hear the shouts of the girls on the hockey-pitch any more. Only the sighing of the tall trees and the crackling of twigs and leaves under my feet, and the wood-pigeons cooing. Everything was overgrown

21

and dank, as if nothing could breathe in there any more. The pond was spread with speckles of green, like a lawn of grass. I almost stepped straight into it. The only break in its surface was where a willow tree trailed its bare branches like skeleton fingers groping into its secret depths. But I sat there for a while, taking in the silence. What little sunlight there was came low and broken through the branches, touching the small insects that droned heavily round me. I felt completely cut off from the school.

'And then I heard it.

'It was a crackle of twigs at first, like a bird moving in the branches. Then a voice, as soft and soothing as a wood-pigeon's.

' "Miss Julie!" it cooed. "Miss Julie!"

'I listened hard. The sound was so gentle that I couldn't be sure of the words at all; or whether in fact I had actually heard anything.

'Nothing.

'I started to make my way back, and then the voice came again. "Miss Julie! Miss Julie!" Soft, and then louder, and then dying away into nothingness. "Miss Julie . . ."

' "Who is it?" I shouted, but my voice was shaking so much that the words hardly broke.

'I began to push my way through the shrubbery, and then suddenly behind me was the voice again, and the sound of a light splash, coming from the pond where no fish lived to leap. I turned round, and there, floating on the dull green surface, was a handful of bright wild flowers.

'I didn't speak to a soul that afternoon. I got through my lessons somehow, though my head was whirling with memories of what had happened in the glen. I didn't go to school the next few days, though my mum didn't know. I spent one day in the park and the next day looking round the big shops in town. But gradually everything died down – I persuaded myself that I really had heard wood-pigeons cooing, and that the wild flowers had been trailing down from the banks of the pond. I went back to school, and everyone was nice to me, and I spent lunchtime that day watching the house netball match. But when I got back to the cloakroom I found that my scarf was missing. I knew I hadn't taken it out with me. I couldn't think what to do. One of the girls said "Why don't you go and ask St Antony where it is?" So, just for a laugh, I did. You wouldn't understand these things, but we Catholics have got a saint for everything, which is quite convenient, and St Antony is the patron saint for finding things. His statue is in a long, green-tiled passage in the basement of the convent. St Antony's passage, we call it. We do needlework down there, all lined up in a long row, with Mother Alberta at the top reading from the Lives of the Saints to us. Anyway, I went off down St Antony's Passage, and sure enough, there was the statue of St Antony with my school scarf draped round his neck. He did look funny! I knew someone had done it for a joke and I was pleased about it because I thought it must have been because they liked me – but when I hooked it down I realised that the joke had been turned against me, for woven into the tassels of the scarf were wild flowers from the glen.

What did it mean? All the memories of that dreadful afternoon in the glen came flooding back to me.

'And then ... I heard the voice again.

'A gentle, cooing wood-pigeon voice ... "Miss Julie. Miss Julie ..." And though it was as soft as a whisper it echoed round and round the long tiled passage. "Who is it?" I shouted, and ran to the corner of St Antony's passage to look down the next one, but there was no-one in sight. The passage was in total darkness. I turned back to look at the statue, and there it came again, "Miss Julie, Miss Julie ..." And then it seemed to come from both ends of the passage at once, over and over again, echoes tumbling round and round and over and under each other like water stumbling over stones.'

Julie paused for a moment. We sat in silence, listening to the dry crackling of the fire. Outside, light, frosted rain tapped the window-pane, like gentle fingers. We waited for her to continue.

'I suddenly forced my legs to move and ran down the passage and up the stairs to my classroom. I was too breathless and frightened to speak, and Mother Alberta couldn't get a word of sense out of me. She sent me straight to Mother Agnes, the headmistress. She has a little study next to the chapel, but when I got there she wasn't in. There was nobody around at all. I couldn't face the thought of going back to class, so I decided to sit in the chapel and wait for her. I knew I would hear Mother Agnes when she came back to her study.

'I felt much better when I was sitting in the chapel. It was very peaceful. There was very little natural light coming through the stained glass windows, because it

24

was quite a dull day. There's a red candle that always burns, you know, day and night, and then there were lots of little candles by the altar, that the nuns had lit after Mass, all fluttering and flickering in the shadows. I just sat in one of the benches, waiting. The scent of polish and incense and flowers, and the silence, and the little flames shivering, just made me want to go to sleep. I closed my eyes . . .

'"Oh no," I breathed. "The voices . . ."

'It was so gentle, at first. Softer than a sigh. It made no more sound than the whispering of the candle flames. "Miss Julie . . ." It just came and went, like a breath, and I strained to hear it again, thinking I had imagined it. "Miss Julie . . ." It came, like the candles fluttering: "Miss Julie! Miss Julie!" and gradually getting louder and louder, till suddenly the chapel wasn't a place of peace any more but was full of long leaping shadows and tall statues leaning towards me and voices swirling round and round like the wind and I rushed down the aisle and through the door and past Mother Agnes and out into the drive towards the gates. I turned round, once, and there running behind me was a nun with her arms full of wild flowers and she called my name and I screamed and ran for the road and saw the car – too late! and slammed into the side of it while the wild flowers showered over me.'

It was Kevin who put the light on, and his jacket, and stood with his hand on the door knob ready to run out into the night.

'I don't believe a word of it!' he said, his voice

trembling. 'You've made it all up!'

'I've made none of it up,' said Julie emphatically. 'There's not a word of a lie in that.'

'Oh, come on, Julie. There must be more to it than that,' I said. 'You wouldn't still be going to the convent school after all that!'

Julie drank down the last of the ginger beer thirstily. 'It was Mother Agnes who sorted it all out,' she said at last. 'In fact, she'd caught the two girls sneaking down the choir stairs just after I ran out of the chapel.'

'What, they'd been doing the voices?'

'Yes. Their stupid idea of a joke. They got sent to another school.'

'And they did the trick with St Antony's statue?'

'Yes. I suppose it was a bit green of me to fall for that – but it was really scary down there in that passage ...'

26

'I bet it was,' I said. 'But what about the nun who ran down the drive after you?'

'With the wild flowers in her arms?' Julie looked a bit embarrassed. 'That was Mother Stanislaus ... She'd been weeding the flowerbeds in the drive, and had run after me to see what had happened.'

Kevin was sitting down again now, his face back to its normal colour. 'So there isn't a ghost in the glen after all.'

'Well, I don't know about that,' said Julie. 'Those two girls denied they'd ever been in the glen. They absolutely refused to admit it. And I'll tell you one thing ... I'll never go near that pond again, as long as I live.'

3. The White Queen

Kevin had been going to see Mrs Wilson since he was six years old. It all started because his mum's friend Pat came over for the day with her little boy Steven, and Steven told him that he had just been given a kitten. Kevin was impressed and envious – the only pets he had ever had were a gerbil that escaped up a gas flue and a hamster that choked on a piece of Lego. He didn't think he even knew any cats, except for the scraggy black one that lived up near the school, and that one was so sick of having its tail pulled that it arched its back and spat every time a child came near it.

Steven suggested that they knocked on people's doors to find out if anyone in the street had a cat that Kevin could play with, and they did just that, side by side, timidly knocking and patiently standing until the fifth door they tried was opened to them. They waited a long time after they heard a voice calling 'Wait a minute!' Steven kept on knocking until the door was opened, ever so slightly, and an old lady looked down at them in annoyance.

'Well, what was all that banging about?'

'He wants to know if you've got a cat,' said Steven.

Kevin was looking at the old lady's hand that trembled on the door post: the dry, freckled skin stretched over the bony fingers, the distorted joints of the knuckles showing white, the broken black finger nails.

'What if I have?'

'He wants to know if he can play with it.'

'Does he now?' And the old lady suddenly bent down and thrust her face up close to Kevin's, so that he felt her wispy, dark grey hair on his face and smelt her faint, sickly, sweetish old-woman's smell.

'Well, he'd better come in then.' And the hand that trembled on the door post groped for the stick that was propped against the wall, and the old lady turned slowly, swivelling on the ball of one slippered foot. She shuffled the other round, and limped across the hall into the dark room opposite.

Steven nudged Kevin, who had changed his mind about cats, and they followed her in silence and hung back in the doorway of the room while she struggled with the dark green curtains and eventually drew them back to let daylight into the room. It smelt of sour milk and newspapers. She leaned heavily on the table that was scattered with books and papers and unwashed dishes, and swung up her walking stick, pointing it first at Kevin and then at the cat, which was blinking sleepily from the depths of the only armchair.

'You can play with him,' she said, and eased herself carefully onto a high-seated chair.

Kevin walked across the room as if he was going to the dentist's. He knelt down and stroked the cat silently.

29

His skin shrank when he felt the rough touch of the cat's tongue on the palm of his hand. He let the claws stretch and drag on the sleeve of his jumper.

The room was soundless, except for the heavy ticking of the clock and the cat's low purr. Kevin fondled and stroked the cat, rubbing his hand again and again over its ear to watch it flick it back with a shake of its head. Once or twice he looked up and gazed round the room at the glass bookcase filled with dark books, the high, cluttered mantelpiece with its photographs of soldiers and wide-eyed girls, the white-faced clock, the bundled dressing gown and night-dress by the fire, but when his eyes met the old lady's he turned away quickly to the cat. She was leaning forward in her chair, her hands clasped over the crook of her walking-stick and her chin resting on her hands; and her eyes were very bright.

Steven stayed in the doorway, following the bumpy pattern on the grimed brass finger plate with his thumb-nail. Eventually he whispered with a squeak, coughed, cleared his throat, and tried again.

'Come on Kev. He's got to go now, Mrs.'

Immediately Kevin stood up and the two boys raced out of the house, down the alley-way and up to Kevin's, where they shouted and punched each other and fell noisily into the kitchen.

The two mums were both on their hands and knees on the floor picking up pins from a spilt pin-box. They both had a row of pins sticking out of their mouths, and when Kevin's mum spoke to him her row collapsed and hung from her bottom lip like hedgehog spikes.

'Mind your feet! Mind that pin-box! You great clumsy ... where do you two think you've been?'

Kevin dive-bombed onto the settee.

'Mum, guess what! I've found a cat to play with!'

And he had been calling on the old lady ever since.

It was a long time, though, before he exchanged any words with her at all. At first he just knocked until she opened the door, followed her silently into the room, and sat on the floor stroking the cat while the old lady watched him or hunched herself over a book. She read greedily, pulling at her lips with her deformed fingers and sucking in her saliva. She never spoke or looked up when he left, and only the cat, stretching and blinking, escorted him to the door.

The first words Kevin ever spoke to the old lady were 'Where is he?' She had led him into the room, as usual, and his gaze had followed her raised stick to the familiar, empty chair.

'Where's your cat?' He felt very uncomfortable.

'That's just it,' she said. She eased herself into her chair. 'He's not my cat at all, only sleeps here, has his food here, thinks he owns the place.' She giggled, like a little girl, with her hand to her mouth. 'But he's not my cat. Oh no!'

Kevin wasn't sure what to do now. He only came to play with the cat – how could he stay if the cat wasn't there? He looked towards his escape route and was reassured to see that the door was still ajar. He struggled with his shyness, while the old lady watched him.

'But where is he?' he asked at last.

And so they talked. The old lady told him how the cat had first come to her, two years before, a tiny kitten in the rain, mewing and shivering and drenched to the skin on her windowsill, and how she had brought it in and fed it and warmed it by the fire and let it sleep all night on the big armchair. The next day the home help, Mrs Harris, had taken a post-card saying 'Kitten found' down to the post office, and put it in the window there, but no-one had come. The kitten had stayed for two weeks, gradually taking over the whole house.

'The first time he left me, I cried like a baby.' She nodded at him, as though expecting him to be surprised. 'Mrs Harris had to take another note down to the post office, saying "Kitten lost", though we knew that he'd probably gone back to the people who owned him, and who must have quite given him up.'

'But he came back?'

Yes, he had come back, and gone away, and come back again, like a husband in the navy, expecting to see his food and his chair by the fire waiting for him as usual. And he always came back when it rained.

'You mark my words,' said old Mrs Wilson, glancing through the window at the overcast sky. 'He'll be back before the day's out.'

It was seven o'clock that night when it began to rain. Kevin heard it spitting down the chimney onto the fire. He looked at his parents anxiously; at his dad, cutting his toenails on the hearth; at his mum, sitting on the carpet close to the fire, reading. If he said a word his mum would look up at the clock and say 'Come on, Kevin, bedtime.' Nothing would have persuaded her to

32

let him go up the street in the dark to Mrs Wilson's house.

He shuffled rather than walked into the hall, as though he was still sitting down really. He didn't even dare put his coat on. He opened the door stealthily and ran as fast as his legs would carry him across the street and up to Mrs Wilson's. 'Kevin!' He heard his mother shouting. 'Just you come back here at once!' He stopped, panting, under the lamp-post at the end of Mrs Wilson's passage. He was just in time to see a curled white tail twisting round the crack of the kitchen door, and to hear Mrs Wilson giggling, 'Come on Mr Dabs. Come and get dry.'

The door closed, and he turned to see his mother running towards him, her slippers slapping on the wet road.

'Kevin, what on earth do you think you're doing?'

'I only came to see if Mr Dabs got home all right, Mum.'

His mother made a tutting noise to show that she was cross, but she squeezed his hand tightly as she walked him back home to bed.

After that it didn't seem to matter any more whether Mr Dabs was there or not when Kevin called round to Mrs Wilson's. He loved to play with the cat, to rub his face in his thick warm fur and feel the cat's paws dabbing his head, his hard little nose and sandpaper tongue nuzzling his neck, his small body throbbing with the vibrations of his purr. But he was often missing, especially in the warmer weather, often for days on end. Kevin would sit for hours talking to Mrs Wilson. He

33

usually called in on his way home from school, when he knew that the home help, Mrs Harris, with all her fuss and gossip, would be out of the way.

As he grew older Kevin became aware of Mrs Wilson's great loneliness. 'Young people can choose who they have for friends,' she used to say, 'but old people have to be grateful for whoever comes to the door. That's why I let two grubby little boys in one day.' But Kevin felt she'd rather have him than Mrs Harris to talk to, any day. 'I never get used to the quiet, when the radio's gone off at night. Not since *he* died.' He was one of the handsome soldiers on the mantelpiece, smiling steadily out of the past, and he had died thirty years ago.

Kevin hated her to talk like this. It made him feel uncomfortable, as if he had no right to be young.

They both liked reading. Sometimes Kevin would bring her a book of his own choice from the school library, and they would take it in turns to read aloud. Then she would get really animated. She never kept her hands still when she was reading, and her twisted trembling fingers would jab and stab the air to give expression to the words on the page. At other times, when he was reading, she would nod and laugh and sigh, according to the mood of the story, and her eyes would be bright. But sometimes she would be very still, and he would stop reading, and stare at her in horror as her head rolled back against the chair and her crumpled hands slid across her knee. He would just watch her, not daring to move.

And she would suddenly wake up, with a surprised look at him, as if he were a stranger in her house, and

he would hastily take up his reading again with his heart racing, the words tumbling awkwardly because of his uneven breath, and after a while she would struggle out to the kitchen to make them both a cup of hot Bovril 'for strength'.

The summer before he moved to the Upper School Kevin went camping with the scouts. He'd never been away from home before. When camp was finished his brother Mike, who was out of work, came to fetch him and took him to his grandparents in Liverpool, and his mum and dad picked him up from there a week later to take him to the caravan in Anglesey for the family holiday. Mum's friend Pat was there too, with Steven and Robert and Caroline. He was away from home for the whole summer. The weeks stretched on endlessly; it was the hottest summer he could remember. And then suddenly it was over. They drove up through a bleak and blustery Wales and into a dull, cold wet England. He sat in the back of the Morris with Mike, staring out at the strange squat houses that suddenly seemed so unfamiliar now, when a sudden feeling like sickness swept over him.

'Oh, no!'

'What's the matter?'

'I've just remembered. I never wrote to Mrs Wilson.'

'Oh Kevin!' His mother turned round from the front seat. 'Not even a card? Well, isn't that mean of you!'

'I couldn't help it, could I? I forgot, that's all.' But he felt ashamed, as if he had let Mrs Wilson down. He scowled out of the window, his cheeks burning.

They drove along in silence for a while.

36

'Take her one of your sticks of rock,' his dad suggested.

'And keep your fingers crossed that her new false teeth have arrived,' said Mike. He always said daft things.

But when Kevin went round to Mrs Wilson's the next day he was let in by Mrs Harris.

'Colour of you!' she said. 'And look at the size of you! Just look where your trousers are up to – you've got legs right up to your bottom.' Kevin squirmed. She was worse than his Auntie Lil. 'She's in there, in bed, so don't make a noise, and don't stay long because the doctor's coming soon.'

Mrs Wilson slept downstairs in what she still called the parlour. It was very dark, with the heavy blue curtain only slightly parted. The furniture was bulky and of very dark wood – a piano with candle-holders on it, a roll-top desk, a marble-topped dresser – but taking up most of the room was a large bed, rough with tumbled clothes. She was asleep when Kevin went in, her mouth slightly open, so that her breath came in sharp little snorts, but as he moved cautiously across the narrow crack of light that knifed through the window she opened her eyes and lifted her hands feebly.

'Hello, Mrs Wilson.'

'So you've come back.'

'I've brought you a present. Some peppermint rock.' He remembered what Mike had said about the false teeth but it didn't seem funny any more.

'I thought you'd forgotten all about me.'

'No.' He turned away, ashamed, and resentful that she should try to make him feel guilty. What was a rotten post-card, anyway? She reached with trembling hands for the glass of water by her bed and he automatically picked it up for her and held it to her lips while she clasped her dry shaking hands around his. There was a strange smell around her.

'What's the matter with you, Mrs Wilson?'

'Matter? It's old age that's the matter, that's what. Catching up with me at last.'

Her voice was whining, like a small child's, and he hated her for it.

'Nobody comes to see me now, Kevin. I lie here all day, and nobody comes to see me.'

'Would you like me to fetch you a library book?'

'You'd have to read it to me. I can't see to read any more. It makes me tired.'

'I'll go now. I'll fetch you one.' Anything to get out. He hated to see her lying there, with her hair wispy and untidy on the pillow, and her twisted fingers fidgeting with the grey edges of her sheet. She was old, she was old. She wasn't Mrs Wilson any more.

'Kevin.'

'Yes?' He paused, on his way out.

'Is it raining yet?'

'Yes.'

'Good. Mr Dabs will be home soon.'

Mrs Harris winked at him grimly from the kitchen.

'That mangy old cat,' she whispered. 'She's driven me mad, asking about him. I bet it's rained every day this week, and every blinking time she opens her eyes

38

it's "Mrs Harris, Mrs Harris, is it raining yet?" till I could scream.'

'But hasn't Mr Dabs come home?'

'No love, nor will he, and she knows it. He got knocked down weeks ago, not long after you'd gone away it was; great big lorry, charging down the street, no right to be here at all. Can't say I like cats, me, but I wouldn't have wished that on the little thing.'

'But why does she keep asking for him?'

'Well, that's old people for you, Kevin. They don't remember what they don't want to remember, that's for sure. Driving me mad, she is.'

Kevin ran out and up the entry, across the street and up to the main road. He couldn't bear to be in the house any longer, with its strange smell of sickness, and Mrs Harris' busy prattling and the sighs and snorts from Mrs Wilson's dark parlour. The road was full of Saturday shoppers, moving slowly with loaded bags or standing in small groups gossiping. He dodged between them, swerving round parked cars and swinging round lamp-posts. He bumped into a pram and backward-danced his apology, and charged, at last, into the pet shop, flinging the door open wide and setting up a chatter and scurry among the cages with the violence of his entry. He leaned on the counter, gasping.

Mr Totley was a slow man. He was serving a customer with oats, and measured them out, scoop by scoop, with meticulous care. There was activity all round him: bright budgies swinging and hopping, hamsters and mice fussing, and, in the huge green aquarium, brilliant fish drifting and shivering. There was a large jar of

squirming baby hamsters, and some mournful spaniel puppies, tumbling and treading on each other in a tight group. And at the back was a white rabbit. She seemed to be completely motionless except for the trembling of her fine whiskers, and she watched Kevin quietly. He wanted to touch her. He bent down under the counter flap, met Mr Totley's knee, backed out, and straightened up.

'No you don't.'

And with irritating slowness Mr Totley brushed the spilled oats off the counter, re-arranged the paper bags, and restocked the shelf of fish-food.

Kevin's eyes kept returning to the white, still rabbit.

'Yes?'

'I've come for a cat.'

'A cat?'

'I want a white cat with black paws. It's for an old lady.'

'We don't have cats here. We sometimes have kittens at six weeks old, but they get bought straight off. We don't sell cats.'

Mr Totley sneezed suddenly, making the budgies jump. He was allergic to oat flakes.

'Now get along home,' he snapped suddenly from inside his handkerchief as the shop door clanged open and a group of adults came in. Small boys ogling at rabbits could hang about all day, under your feet.

Kevin went next door to the sweet shop, then sidled back again. He stood with his back to the pet-shop so Mr Totley wouldn't recognise him, and just turned his head slightly so that he had the white rabbit in focus. Like a big white queen she was, serene in all that bustle. Queenie, he thought.

He suddenly pushed open the shop door again.

'How much for the white rabbit?' he shouted.

Mr Totley shook his head at the man he was serving, and tapped at the board of prices propped up against the till.

'I thought it was a cat you was after.'

Kevin was busily doing calculations. He'd some money in the post office still, that his mum hadn't let him take on holiday. And he could ask his dad to advance him a week's pocket money.

'Will you save her for me, Mr Totley?' he shouted.

The man seemed not to hear him. He was weighing out again, and breathing sharply between closed teeth, so that his breath whistled. His eyes were streaming.

'You tell me you've got a rabbit hutch,' he said quietly, without looking up. 'And then I'll think about selling you this rabbit. Will that be all, sir?' And he smiled across to his customer, his white teeth gleaming.

Kevin sank down moodily against the side of the shop. His legs stuck out over the pavement, so that passersby had to step over him and push their shopping trolleys and prams round him. Suddenly he jerked himself up and ran into the shop, thrusting his head up towards Mr Totley.

'My Uncle Billy's got a hutch,' he said. 'I know he has. They keep it in their kitchen with tins of polish in it.'

But Mr Totley wasn't even listening.

It was two miles to Uncle Billy's house, over the railway lines. Kevin charged off again. He passed Julie and Sally on their way to the baths. Julie's towel was unrolling under her arm and the straps of her costume were dangling down behind her. Normally he would have grabbed hold of them and yanked the costume out and gone racing off with it twirling round his head and Julie screeching after him. His head was bursting. If he was going to get to Uncle Billy's and get the hutch back home and get his post office money out, and find his dad at the allotments for an advance on his pocket money, and get back to the pet shop for Queenie before it closed, he was going to need some help.

'Hey, Julie, do us a favour, will you?'

'No chance,' she said, not even looking at him. Her Barbie and his Mike had fallen out again, and she was taking sides.

'Hey, Sally, will you?'

'Do me one, and get lost,' she said.

And they crossed over the road, with their hair bouncing and Julie's costume trailing behind her.

'Hope you drown yourselves!' Kevin shouted after them, and smirked triumphantly as Julie's costume tumbled out and lay on the road like a little blue and white spotted animal squashed by the traffic. Julie and Sally marched on.

His Uncle Billy gave him a lift back to the shop, and the White Queen was carried out with great ceremony to the hutch in the car. She watched quietly. Uncle Billy carried the hutch to Mrs Wilson's back door, and Kevin lifted out the White Queen gently. She was heavy and soft, and although her nose quivered anxiously she remained quite still in his arms. It was Kevin's proudest moment, when he carried Queenie through into Mrs Wilson's kitchen in his arms.

Mrs Harris was at the sink, washing sheets. She advanced at him, up to her elbows in bubbles of soap.

'Where the Harry Blazes do you think you're going with that thing?'

He marched past her, resolutely, to the door that led to Mrs Wilson's parlour.

'I've brought a present for Mrs Wilson.'

Mrs Harris beat him to the door. She stood holding her arm across the doorway like the bar of a gate. Trickles of soapy water ran down the door-post.

'You're not going in there with no animals,' she hissed. 'I'm not having no rabbits running round that room. I've only just cleaned it.'

'But I've got a hutch for it. It'll go at the bottom of her bed. It won't make a mess.'

'Fur would get up her nose.'

'No it wouldn't. See.' He pushed Queenie up towards Mrs Harris's face.

'See, it doesn't go up your nose, does it?'

The home help rubbed her nose irritably. 'She doesn't want no rabbits in there, thumping about.'

'She'd be able to watch it.'

'She hasn't got time for watching things. She's poorly.'

From inside the parlour Mrs Wilson's voice grumbled peevishly.

'What is it?'

'It's a rabbit, Mrs Wilson,' Kevin shouted excitedly.

'Rabbit? Have you got a bit of ham to go with it?'

'There you are, you see,' said Mrs Harris, triumphantly. 'That's all they're fit for, them things. Stewing!' She shuddered violently. 'Take it away. I can't abide them things. They nip.'

Kevin could feel the tears of frustration stinging his eyes. He wanted to throw the rabbit at Mrs Harris, shouting 'Bite her, bite her. Kill!' Instead he stumbled out of the room, burying his head in the soft white fur. Queenie was warm and heavy in his arms.

He went round to the front of the house, to Mrs Wilson's front parlour window, and peered in. The curtains were only slightly open, and the room was in darkness. It was a long time before he could make out any of the swimming shapes, but when at last he saw Mrs Wilson she was lying on the bed with her mouth open, watching him. She lifted up her hand feebly and waved at him. He held up the White Queen so that her face was next to his own, and old Mrs Wilson smiled, and closed her eyes, and slept.

Kevin kept Queenie in his own back yard. Every day he carried her in his arms up to Mrs Wilson's house and held her up at the window for her. She always woke up when they came, and smiled weakly at them. One day it was raining, and they stood outside, shivering and wet, till Mrs Harris opened the kitchen door and called up the passage to them, 'You'd better come in for half a minute.'

Kevin walked through to the parlour holding the White Queen up in front of him, so that her twitching nose led the way through the door. Mrs Wilson giggled.

'Come in, Mr Dabs,' she said. 'Come in and get dry.'

When the old lady died a few days later, Kevin was very sad, but not really surprised. He had known that she wasn't going to get better.

He looked after her rabbit for her, though. She lived at the bottom of his yard, silent and peaceful, for years and years. He painted her name on Uncle Billy's hutch: 'The White Queen', in big red letters, and, in brackets, 'Queenie'.

But she was always known to all of us kids in the street as Mrs Wilson's cat.

4. Weird George

Weird George moved into old Mrs Wilson's house with his mum and dad. When we came home from school one day the removal van was in the road. We all dropped our bags and coats on the pavement and settled down against Julie's wall to watch. Kevin passed round some tomato ketchup sandwiches he'd got left over from dinner time, and when Julie came home from the convent school she went over to Mrs Marriot's with a jug and bought some lemonade to share round. There were still pips swimming round in it and little fleshy buds of lemon, and it was all sharp and made you screw your eyes up and grind your teeth together. We loved it. We were all mad when our mums called us in to tea. We didn't want to miss anything.

Mrs Wilson's house had stood empty for weeks, since she died. Kevin was still a bit funny about the place, as if there was an evil spell on it or something. He had gone in to see all the flowers in the front parlour, before the funeral men came, and later on, when the funeral cars had passed down the road and we'd all drawn our curtains out of respect for the dead, he'd sat outside drawing pictures in chalk on the pavement. He looked vicious. I'd peeped out through the curtains at him, and my mum said he was a wicked boy not to stay indoors till all the cars had passed. But I knew a bit how he felt.

It was funny how we all somehow expected another old lady to move in, but it was soon obvious from the furniture that was carried in that it was someone with modern taste, and that there was at least one child – we knew that because of the bright blue bike that was carried in. Kevin grinned all over his face when he saw that it was a boy's bike. What with me and Marie and Julie he'd had enough of girls. There were the snotty-nosed twins, Eddie and Leslie, who lived down by the laundry, but he never bothered with them. I can't say I blamed him. You could smell their feet a mile off.

The new people arrived the next day, and immediately set about turning Mrs Wilson's house inside out. A skip came from the council, and was gradually filled up with all sorts of old carpets and broken fire-places and books.

Her books! Kevin was horrified. He used to sneak them out of the skip, just the odd book or two, and stuff them under his jumper and run off home with them. Marie started sneaking books off too but her mum made her put them back.

One day Kevin got some photographs that had just been thrown on the pile. There was a soldier with dark brown eyes and a little trim moustache. He said that was Mr Wilson. And a girl with her dark hair smoothed back, in a long tight dress. He said that was Mrs Wilson when she was young. I thought it was beautiful. I couldn't believe that the old lady that I could only just remember had ever really looked like that.

The new boy at the house was called George. He was weird. He used to wobble up and down the road on his bright blue bike, looking at you. His face was very white and his eyes were staring. He'd got little tufts of hair on his chin. It made me feel strange just to look at him. If I went up to him he would just stand still and stare at me – his eyes seemed to look right through me so that I wanted to look round and see what it was that he was looking at behind. He never smiled or spoke. Just stared. It made me want to run away. He didn't seem able to walk properly at all. His legs seemed to jerk in the middle, with his knees giving a little click with every step he took. And his arms would just hang down, with his fat red hands on the end of them as if they had nothing to do with the rest of his body at all. He was always there, wobbling about on his bike or clicking down the street, watching us. He was weird.

He went to our school, but he didn't seem to come every day. He was in a different class from me and Kevin and Marie, but we sometimes used to see him in the yard, sitting all by himself near the railings, just staring. It wasn't long before some of the girls started making fun of him.

'Georgy Porgy, pudding and pie,
  Kissed the girls and made them cry.'

And he would suddenly lunge out at them and send them screaming like sea-gulls across the yard, while he ran after them with his arms stretched out in front of him, trying to catch them. He never did, of course. He couldn't even run the same way as he was looking.

He came to school one day with his hair all shaved on one side. It looked really strange because most of his hair was brown and spiky, and this little patch was all crozzled and ginger. Julie told me that night that she had heard his mum shouting at him in the yard – he'd put his head down to the cooker to listen to the gas flame, and he'd nearly burnt his ear off.

'Mum, that kid's weird!' I said at teatime. 'Do you know what he did today ...'

'Now don't you go making fun of him, Bee, do you hear me?' She nearly jumped down my throat, and I went bright red. I'd expected her to laugh at him too. 'He's got a mother who's worried sick about him. The doctor wants him sent away to a special school, and she won't hear of it. That's why she's moved here, because the kids in the other place plagued the life out of him. Just leave him alone.'

I looked out of the window, feeling miserable. It wasn't often my mum shouted at me. It wasn't my fault if he was weird.

I went out to Julie's and stood outside waiting for her to change out of her uniform. George was sitting on his step next door, with a gold-fish bowl stuck in front of him. Right, I thought. I'll go and talk to him. I went and stood by him, while he trailed his hand in the gold-fish water.

'What are you doing, George?' I asked. I felt as if I was talking to one of Julie's little brothers.

'I'm catching fish,' he said thickly. It was the first

49

time I had ever heard his voice. It wasn't all up and down squeaky like Kevin's is now. It was already nearly like a man's voice. I watched him while he wriggled his fingers about in the bowl, and then he brought a goldfish out and laid it on the step beside him. It jumped about for a bit, making a clapping sound on the concrete, and then heaved itself heavily sideways, gasping helplessly.

'Put it back, George,' I said firmly. 'Put it back or it will die.'

'No,' he said, putting his hands over it and looking up at me defiantly. 'It's mine. It's my fish.'

Julie came and joined me, and I told her what George had done.

'That's wicked and cruel,' she said. 'What harm has that fish ever done you?'

'I don't like it,' he said. He brought a penknife out of his pocket and flicked it open. He leered up at us. Then he held the fish between his thumb and first finger and very gently and firmly sliced it across with his knife. The fish's cold eye stared up at us. We couldn't say anything, either of us. I'd watched my Mum filleting plaice sometimes, that she'd bought half-alive still off Fish-May's cart down by the slipway - chop the head off, wash the blood out, prise out the bones like a long delicate comb - but I'd never been sickened by that like I was at the sight of this weird lad slicing up his goldfish. The three of us looked down in silence at the slimy pieces of fish glistening on the steps, and then suddenly Julie said, 'Hey George, your mum's coming!'

We turned to run off, as guilty as he, but George's

hand streaked out, quick as lightning, picked up the fish pieces, and popped them in his mouth. He stared at us thoughtfully, chewing.

We ran up the road, nearly laughing, nearly sick. Julie started giggling.

'What if it all joins up like a worm and starts flapping about inside him?'

'Do you think it'll poison him?'

We told Kevin about it and he looked very solemn.

'Our Mike knows someone who ate a bee,' he said.

'On purpose?'

'Well, not exactly. He was eating a jam sandwich and the bee flew in with it.'

I didn't wait to hear what had happened next. I'd had enough.

I wish Mum had never made me talk to George, though. He never left me alone after that. He followed me round everywhere, like a puppy being taken for a walk, just a few feet behind me. I know Marie and I used to do that at school, following the lads that we liked round the yard, but we always pretended that we weren't, really. We'd have died rather than let on. George gave me the creeps, he really did. He was weird. Sometimes when he was following me I'd stop dead, so he nearly smacked right into me, and I'd say 'Have you seen enough?' or 'Go and play on the railway lines for half an hour,' but something about his sad eyes made me feel sorry. He'd stuff his big red hands in his pockets helplessly and walk away, and I would feel as if I'd just kicked a dog.

But it didn't seem to make any difference. He started

51

giving me presents. At first he used to push them through the letter-box, just little things wrapped up in corners of newspaper – a pencil sharpener, a stick of liquorice – things like that. I never let on to him that I'd got them, and I saved them all in my drawer. If Mum picked the little presents up before I did, I used to pretend that I didn't know anything about them. I didn't tell Marie about them, or even Julie. I thought they might laugh at me or make fun of George about them and I didn't want them to do that. I did tell Kevin about them, one day, and he was really strange. He went scarlet. I thought at first I'd made a mistake and that he'd sent them, not George, though I couldn't imagine why he would do a thing like that. Then I realised that he wasn't embarrassed, he was angry.

'You shouldn't take them off him, Bee. Send them back,' he said. He was aiming little pebbles at the sparrows on the wall, like he always did, but this time he looked as if he really meant to knock them off, like coconuts.

'He's all right, Kevin,' I said. 'He's harmless.'

'He's weird,' said Kevin. 'You don't want to have anything to do with him.'

'I don't,' I said. 'I just feel sorry for him, that's all. He's lonely.'

'I'm not surprised. The only person he ever talks to is himself.' And he did an imitation of George, peering down at his fingers and muttering away. I laughed, like I always did, but I felt a bit ashamed. It was easy to make fun of George.

That afternoon I was walking round the schoolyard

with Marie, conscious of George's knees clicking away behind me, when Marie said, 'I think Georgy Porgy's got something for you,' and I turned round to see George standing with his hand stretched out towards me, holding one of his newspaper parcels. I felt really embarrassed, but I didn't want to hurt his feelings. I shook my head at him and turned away, but he dodged in front of me and held it out again. Marie was giggling at him, and some of the other girls had stopped to have a look. I felt really sorry for George. I shook my head again, just wishing that one of the gulls flying round would swoop down and carry him off over the railings, and I would never have to be bothered about him again.

'I'm talking to Marie, George,' I said firmly. That helpless look that made me feel so guilty came over him again, and he walked away slowly, brushing past me. As he did so he dropped the little roll of newspaper into my coat pocket, and tapped it down gently. He didn't look at me, just walked on past.

'What's that he's given you?' asked Marie sharply. She never misses a thing. She's like her mum. I can't stand her, really.

'Nothing,' I said. 'He just touched my coat.'

'Have a look in your pocket,' she ordered. 'He put something in, I saw him.'

'No, he hasn't. There's nothing there.' I stuck my hand in my pocket and held the little present. I was dying to know what it was. When the bell went for lessons I dodged out of Marie's way and slipped into the girls' cloakroom. I was just about to open it up when she came in looking for me, so I shoved it in my skirt pocket. I could feel it there all afternoon, waiting to be opened. I really liked George's little presents. They were funny.

I waited till I got home to open it up. I went upstairs as soon as I got in and shut myself in my room. The little parcel felt very light in my hand and part of it was loose, as if it was broken.

'Perhaps it's something he's made in pottery,' I thought, 'and he's gone and dropped it.'

I held it over the bed and shook it out of the newspaper, and as it fell it glinted brightly against the dark cover.

It was a lady's watch.

I picked it up. I could hardly believe it at first. I thought it must be a child's plastic watch with gold paint. I wound it up gently, and the sound was like a cat licking itself softly. I held it to my ear and listened to it ticking, like tiny footsteps racing. It was beautiful. It had a bracelet strap that stretched to go over my hand and then closed up together on my wrist. I loved it. I'd never had a watch.

My mother called me down to tea and I pushed it guiltily to the back of my drawer. After tea I ran up, and without even looking grabbed the watch from the drawer, wrapped it back up in the newspaper, and ran outside. I knew I couldn't keep it. George wobbled past on his bike, and when I started to follow him he drove the pedals down and raced to the end of the street. I panted after him, pretending I was going to meet my dad off the train, in case any of the others saw me.

'George!' I shouted at last, feeling silly. 'Hold on, you

great lobster!' And he suddenly slammed his feet down so hard that the front of his bike swung up and he slid down on his backside.

I held the watch out to him.

'Don't you like it?' he asked.

'Of course I do, it's beautiful. But I can't keep it, George.'

'Why not?'

'Well, I can't. It's ... too nice.'

'That's daft,' he said thoughtfully. 'It's for you.'

'George, is it your mother's watch?'

A train was rumbling up, slowly, and it gathered speed as it passed us and drowned out George's reply. He didn't seem to notice and just went on talking, and I watched the little black hole of his mouth opening and closing over his crooked baby teeth, and thought of his gold-fish going down. And all the time he was talking he was waving to the people in the train.

'He's weird,' I thought.

'... my money.' He finished, as the train rattled off.

'You bought it with your money?' I asked. I couldn't believe it.

'Yes, I bought it for you, Bee,' he said.

'Well, I can't keep it.' I offered it to him again, but I wasn't so sure this time. I had been certain that he'd taken it from his mum and that he'd be quite pleased to have it back again. I was quite put out to see how hurt he'd looked. But he couldn't have bought it for me, surely.

'Take it back, George.' I didn't sound very convincing. But how could I wear it, anyway? Everyone would want to know where I'd got it from. I pushed it back to him again. 'Go on George, please.'

He sort of sneered at me, as though he'd won a victory over me. He swung up on his bike and rode off without looking round. 'Do what you like with it,' he shouted. 'I don't want it.'

I took the watch out of the newspaper and wound it up slowly, listening to it ticking. I walked down the street with my wrist against my ear, and my face a bit screwed up so that if anyone was watching they'd think I'd got earache, and then when I got home I wriggled it off my wrist and slipped it into my pocket. I took it upstairs and pushed it to the back of the drawer. My watch! But I didn't feel easy about it. There was very little I could do with it, really. A couple of times I went down to the railway lines with it and stood on the bridge timing the trains from the station up the track to ours, but I felt silly, because Weird George would always be sitting on his bike on the cinder path, watching me.

I was sitting in assembly one morning behind Marie, plaiting her hair, when Mr Murphy made one of his Serious Announcements. He always drops his voice right down when he has something to say that he really wants you to hear. It's funny how that always makes you listen. It makes my inside go all goose-pimply when he does that.

'... something very serious to report,' he was saying, 'concerning a missing article. A sixth-former has lost a watch recently ...' Then my hands fell from Marie's hair and I leaned forward. I was drenched in a cold

57

sweat, as if I was going to faint. '. . . thinking the watch was merely mislaid, did not report the loss. However, the watch has not turned up, after repeated searchings. Now I am not saying that this watch has been stolen. I am saying that *someone in this school knows something about it*. And this person, whoever he or she may be, can be trusted to come to me, in confidence, and tell me what they know. I give you till the end of the day, before more serious steps are taken.'

There was a buzz of talking round me as Mr Murphy swept off the stage and marched down the hall. I still felt dizzy, and sat with my head down between my hands, and black stars floating in front of my eyes, while row by row the classes moved out. I sat up as Marie's row moved out and suddenly realised that one side of her hair was in a neat little plait sticking out at a right angle from her ear and the other side was all curly as usual. I'd still got her elastic band round my wrist. She'd be mad when she found out.

I went off to singing but the little black notes kept bobbing about like tadpoles in a pond as I tried to focus on them, and I couldn't work my mouth to keep up with the others. I kept thinking about my beautiful watch ticking away amongst my socks. I had to bring it back; it wasn't mine; I couldn't keep it. But what would happen to me? Was I as guilty as George, for receiving stolen goods? Would I get sent away from school? All of a sudden that didn't sound very appealing, after all. But George! And that came hammering through, like a great gong booming in my ears. I knew, absolutely certainly, what would happen to him. He would be sent

58

away. It was just what they'd been waiting for, all those welfare people. They'd take him away from his mum and dad, and they'd put him in a home, and they'd keep him there for the rest of his life. 'He's proved he's not right,' I thought. 'He's proved he can't behave like the rest of us.'

But if I hadn't been nice to him in the first place he'd never have given me the watch. And I could have made him take it back. Or shoved it through his letter box. It was too late now; I was involved. I couldn't just leave it to George to get himself out of it. But I couldn't see what I could do that wasn't going to get Weird George into trouble, and get him sent away from his mum and dad. I thought of him wobbling up and down the street on his blue bike, ringing his bell at the birds – he was all right really. He was harmless. I suppose I even liked him, in a funny sort of way.

It was lucky for me that my mum was out at dinner time. She'd just got herself a job down at the laundry and she ate her sandwiches with the girls. I got the key from under the bin and went in and got my little watch from the drawer. I rubbed its face on my sleeve to make it shine and then held it up to listen to it tick. I wrapped it up in toilet paper and put it in a sweet bag, and then I went back up the hill to the school, holding it in my pocket. I stood in the yard watching George. He was kicking a ball round with a couple of other lads, laughing, and I suddenly realised how we'd all got used to him, and stopped making fun of him, even. What would he be like when they sent him away to a place where everyone was nutty. Even weirder than him?

Then I knew that I couldn't tell Mr Murphy about George. I'd say I'd just found the watch this morning in the toilets. They couldn't prove anything. They'd have the watch back, that was what mattered. I pushed my way past all the others who were hanging round the doorway as if they were waiting for a pop star to come out. Funny how everyone always wants to be in school when they're supposed to be out, and always wants to get out when they're supposed to be in. It was like getting through a rugby scrum, trying to get to the dinner lady, and then I didn't dare tell her that I wanted to see Mr Murphy, because everyone would have known why. I told her I felt sick and I wanted to sit down and wait for Matron, and I suppose I must have looked pretty sick because she let me in straight away. I walked down to Matron's room and hung around for a bit wondering if I was going to be sick, and then I sidled down the corridor to Mr Murphy's office. I couldn't believe it. The door was open; the room was empty. I slipped in and pushed the packet across the table and then I suddenly thought – is it a trap? What if he's standing behind the door watching me? I felt spiders walking all over the back of my head. I made myself turn round. He wasn't there. He wasn't hiding under his desk and he wasn't looking through the window at me. I grabbed a biro from the jar of pens and pencils on the desk and scribbled on the corner of the sweet bag 'MISSING WATCH!' My writing was wobbly enough without having to try to disguise it. Then I raced down the corridor as if a wild elephant was after me, flung open the doors and charged past the dinner lady.

'Better now, love?' she shouted after me, but I was running round the yard like a bat gone crazy. I was really happy. They'd never know now who'd taken the watch, or who'd returned it. I didn't even feel scared any more. The bell went for afternoon school and they all charged in as if free lollies were being given out, and I stood in the middle of the yard on my own with a sudden dread like cold rain soaking into me. Fingerprints! That watch would be covered in them!

I was fretting about it all afternoon. When Julie came round after school I said I had a headache and she looked at me suspiciously. 'What's up?' she asked.

'Nothing,' I said. 'Too much geography.'

She didn't believe me but I couldn't tell her the truth.

She was a Catholic, and I knew she'd say I would have to go to Mr Murphy and tell him everything. It was easy for her. She was like that. I went off to bed but I didn't sleep. I lay awake all night worrying about George being sent away from home. How long did fingerprints last? Would his still be on the watch?

Mr Murphy took assembly again next day. Usually he takes it every other day. He held up his hands for silence and beamed round at us.

'I am pleased to be able to tell you,' he said, 'that the missing watch has been found again.' I glared down at the floor to make it keep still. 'It was handed in to me by the caretaker, and has been identified by the boy who lost it.'

Boy! I nearly stood up and shouted it back at him. Boys don't wear watches like that!

'Curiously, however,' he went on, ignoring me, 'I now have in my possession another watch sent in by a mysterious donor. I think perhaps the owner of the second watch had better come and see me at break.'

I daren't look at George. How could I ever face him again? I kicked round the yard at break, thinking of my little watch wrapped up in toilet paper on the headmaster's desk, and I knew I couldn't go for it. Mr Murphy would never believe that Weird George had bought it for me. There'd be questions, questions, questions, all over the place. And it might still end up with him being sent away from his mum and dad.

And that lovely watch. I wished I could have it back.

I couldn't eat my tea that night, I was so fed up. Mum couldn't get a thing out of me. You just can't start to tell grown-ups about things like that. They get all angry and they never believe you anyway. She was doing her best to cheer me up and suddenly, without realising it, she solved all my problems at once.

'Come on,' she said, 'long string of misery! What do you want me to get you for your birthday next week?'

I slopped my cup down on the table so hard that all the tea slurped over the cloth.

'I know exactly what I want!' I shouted at her, so excited that she forgot to tell me off about the tea stain. 'A watch! I know exactly what make. Oh can I, can I please, Mum?'

She looked doubtful. Watches were expensive.

'Well, if that's what you really want, Bee. I thought a new dress ...'

'No, a watch! It's got to be a watch!'

'Well, you find out how much the one you want is, and if it's more than I want to pay I'll ask Grandad to help out for his present.'

I felt as if a vacuum cleaner had sucked my headache out though my ears.

'Can I have those beans now, Mum?' I said. 'I'm starving!'

I wore my new watch to school a week later. All my friends knew it was a birthday present.

But Weird George grinned at me from across the yard. He pointed to his wrist, and held it up to his ear, as if to say 'I see you've got my watch on.'

And who was I to tell him any different?

5. Toad

Going into Julie's house was a bit like going to a jumble sale when all the best things had been sold. There were five children altogether. Two of them were still babies really, so there were always toys and coloured pencils and potties and that lying round, and the clothes rack was always dripping with nappies and socks. The sideboards and chairs had crumpled heaps of clothes waiting to be ironed, and concertina piles of clothes just ironed. The place was over-run with guinea-pigs too. They had three of them, and they used to let them run round the back room. They were always getting trodden on. If you managed to sit down at all you had to share your chair with the washing or a baby or a guinea-pig, or all three. The walls all had a tide-mark of grubby fingerprints about two feet up, and had dozens and dozens of funny kids' drawings stuck to them, all bright colours and little men and suns and engines and tigers all smiling away. The place wasn't what you'd call dirty, just out of control. I used to love going there, except for that time when Julie got all snobby about getting a scholarship to the convent school.

You've never known such a family for being accident-prone. Her dad used to be a milkman but he had so many bumps in his milk-float that they had to put him on to office work before they ran out of milk-bottles. Her mum fell off the ladder when she was painting the front of the house – Mr Mills suffered from vertigo so he couldn't have done it anyway. Then there was the time that Julie got knocked down outside school – the daft rabbit. On annual fair day the little ones usually came home howling and bloody and sometimes toothless because they'd fallen off or over or into something. But I think the worst time of all was when Julie's big sister Barbie nearly lost two fingers in a machine at the laundry. I remember her running up our street to the hospital. She was shouting with pain and anger, and her face was white. She was holding her right hand over her left hand, and Julie said afterwards that Barbie had picked her fingers up out of the machine and shoved them back into the sockets, but I don't believe that. That's just Julie showing off. Anyway, Barbie came charging down our street, howling, and we all ran to the door to see what was happening. Three other women from the laundry ran after her, still in their work turbans, and one of them was my mum. So I joined in and so did Julie and her brothers, and Kevin, because his brother Mike was Barbie's boyfriend, and we all ran up the road shouting 'What's up, what's up?'. And when we found out we shouted to people who asked us, 'It's all right, she's lost two fingers in the laundry.'

We all stood outside the big door of the hospital, waiting for Barbie to come out. I wondered if Julie was praying for her. She eventually came out with her hand all bandaged up and we all jostled round her like television reporters asking her how it had happened and if she was all right.

'I'm all right,' she said, and two huge tears like bubbles grew and wobbled at the corners of her eyes. 'But the worst thing is, the machine chopped my engagement ring clean in two.' There it was, two little twists of gold that looked as if they didn't belong to each other any more, and a chewed-up stone. We all looked at Kevin, who blushed and said he'd tell Mike about it.

Barbie shook her head and burst into tears.

'That's not the point,' she said. 'I'm sure it's a bad omen.' And we all followed her home in silence, wondering what could be going to happen that was worse than nearly losing two fingers.

Mum went off back to the laundry. It was at the bottom of the street, in front of the railway lines. You could hear it, clattering away, when you went past it, wheezing out steam like an old woman who smoked too much. Lots of the women in our street worked there, but my mum was always complaining about it. She said it was like a working museum, it was so old-fashioned. The afternoon of Barbie's accident she came home early, looking grim. She set about getting the tea ready in silence, and Dad sat watching her, waiting for her to speak.

'Well,' she said at last, not looking at him. 'You can say goodbye to puddings for the time being.'

Dad chewed slowly, watching her.

'What do you mean?'

'I mean we'll be out of pocket, that's what.'

She folded her arms. 'I'm going on strike.'

'You're going where?'

'You heard. I'm going on strike. For better working conditions.'

Dad leaned forward.

'There, do you mean, or here?'

'There, you daft dumpling. At the laundry.'

'Oh, I was going to say.' He buttered himself some bread. 'I thought you meant here. I wondered what you were on about.'

Mum raised her eyebrows at me, but I didn't know what she was on about either. Strikes were men on the news, carworkers and miners, shouting at each other. She pulled out the chair opposite Dad.

'I've pulled the girls out on strike,' she said importantly. 'We're working with machinery that's as old as the hills. It wasn't Barbie's fault, that accident. There's no guard on that machine. And it's noisy in there, everything banging and thumping. No wonder I've no voice left when I get home. It's so noisy there, I have to stop talking sometimes.'

Dad winked at me. 'Imagine that!' he said.

Mum snorted, disgusted with him.

'And the air conditioning's worse than useless. I've that much steam inside me, I must look like a kettle on the boil every time I open my mouth.'

'Well,' said Dad at last. He looked a bit puzzled, as if he couldn't quite make her out. 'You've never been interested in politics before, love.'

'That's not politics, you great cheese sandwich! That's people!' She banged the chair back and ran over the road to Barbie's house. I've never seen Mum so angry before, or Dad so puzzled.

When Mum got up the next morning she put her work apron and turban on in the house, which is a thing she never does.

'Are you going to work, then?' I asked, puzzled.

'I am *not*!' she said grimly.

There was a knock at the door, and two of the women from the laundry came in. They too were wearing clean white overalls and turbans.

'Are you ready, then?' said one of them to Mum. They all looked a bit tense. Mum nodded to them and they all went out together, and as they walked down the street more and more women from the laundry joined them, all dressed in their working clothes. They all nodded to each other grimly and followed Mum down, nobody talking or laughing like they usually did. Barbie came out of her house with Julie. She'd got her hand strapped up now, held on a sling, so that the empty sleeve of her overall hung down uselessly. She looked really tired, as if she'd never slept all night.

'Don't come down the street with us!' she said.

'Why not?' asked Julie. 'What are you going to do?'

'Nothing!' said Barbie.

We ran off down the entry to the next street, then down to the cinder track by the railway, and up onto the railway bridge. We could see right into the laundry yard from there. Some other kids were on the bridge already. Julie had missed her bus, and we'd all probably be late for school, but we had to know what was happening.

They looked really strange, all those women and girls

in white, moving backwards and forwards from group to group like sea-gulls on the beach. They looked as if they didn't know what to do with themselves. Then one of them started speaking; we couldn't hear what she said but the wind blew her voice towards us and I knew it was my mum. All the women had broken their groups and had clustered around her. Suddenly they all started cheering. We saw Barbie stand by Mum and hold up her bandaged hand.

Julie and I started laughing. We were really excited. A train thundered underneath us and we laughed louder, and then started cheering too, and all the other kids on the bridge started joining in.

'Good old Mum!' I shouted, getting carried away, and her voice suddenly boomed out to us from the laundry yard.

'Just you get off to school this minute, Bee, you great lump of porridge!'

Mum and Dad weren't on speaking terms that night. There'd been a reporter down at the laundry that afternoon, and she'd had her photograph taken, along with Barbie. It would be sure to be in the local paper on Friday.

'I'll be a laughing stock,' grumbled Dad.

I couldn't understand it. I thought he would have been proud of her. I went over to see Julie about it and she said that Mike had had a terrible row over the strike with Barbie. He'd been working at the laundry for a month now, as a van driver. It was his fifth job that year, and he reckoned it was the one he'd liked the best. 'And now you've gone and done me out of it!' he'd shouted at her. Julie couldn't help overhearing. You couldn't exactly have a row in private in a house like hers.

'How do you mean, done you out of it?' Barbie had shouted back.

'Use your head, woman! If you girls don't do the laundry, there's none for me to deliver, is there? Can't you see beyond your silly little noses?'

Barbie had burst into tears and said he didn't care about her fingers, and if she'd still got his ring on she'd throw it back at him right now. He'd roared off on his motor-bike and she'd sat among the guinea-pigs and the piles of dirty washing and howled as if two more fingers had dropped off.

Things went on like this for days, but gradually getting worse. Mum got more and more tight-faced, and Dad got more and more irritable, and Barbie got more and more weepy. I stopped being famous at school because my mum had called the strike, and Julie got sick of telling people that Barbie hadn't actually lost two fingers, or the use of her left side, and she hadn't got the creeping gangrene. Occasionally scuffles broke out here and there in the school playground, among kids whose mums worked at the laundry – some would be fighting on the side of the strikers, and some would be fighting to have it called off. Those who were against the strike blamed me – they said that most of the women wanted to go back, really, but that my mum wouldn't let them. Sometimes people banged on the kitchen window as they went past. Kevin and Julie got dragged into it too; some of the older kids thought they ought to try and make Barbie and Mike get together again – if Barbie decided to go back to start saving up for her wedding all the other women would want to start working as well to back her up. The strain on Barbie was terrible. But she knew my mum was right. They had to force the boss to make things better for them at work, and if this was the only way they could do it, they had to stick together and stay out.

The strike wasn't fun any more.

Julie and I were the only ones now who ever went down to watch the strikers lined up outside the laundry, and we didn't always bother to go. We wandered down one evening when the women had all gone home for their tea. We got into the laundry yard and started peering in through the windows, just in case the boss had got any workmen started on clearing the place up. He hadn't, of course. The place looked dreadful, all cluttered up with pipes and machines, and it was painted a nasty seaweedy green. Suddenly a car drew up really quietly behind us. We swung round, ready to run. A fat little man slid out of the car and came smiling over to us. His eyes bulged like little brown marbles, and his skin lay in dry folds over the collar of his shirt. His podgy little hands were shaking.

'I believe you're just the two little girls I was looking for,' he said.

Little girls! I was taller than him, even in my gym shoes.

'Aren't you Barbara's sister?' he asked Julie. She squinted slightly, like she always does when she's nervous, and nodded.

72

'And you're bound to be Mrs Horton's little girl, with those pretty curls.' He rolled his watery marble eyes round to me. I squirmed. I hated being told I looked like my mum, and I hated people noticing my curls.

'Well,' he beamed, so the rolls of dry flesh parted at each side of his mouth, quivering. 'And I'm Mr West.'

Our eyes shot up to the sign over the laundry.

WEST'S WHITES ARE BEST WHITES

'And how's Barbara's hand?' he asked solicitously.

'All right,' said Julie. I could tell she was ready to run.

'She'll be getting married soon, I believe,' he continued.

I was just about to blurt out that the engagement was broken, like the ring, when Julie squinted vaguely in my direction, and I shut up. None of his business, I thought.

'Now then,' he beamed again, 'you could be nice little girls and take a message to Barbara, couldn't you? I'm sure you won't forget. Tell her that Mr West has a little engagement present for her. When she comes back to work. Tell her there'll be a little party for her as well, for her and all her friends at work. And I'm sure you two could come along as well. I'm sure you could. You tell her; it's all waiting for her. When she comes back to work. Goodbye now!' One of the marbles disappeared behind a fold of skin; his mouth pushed the flabs of his cheeks aside. We watched him waddle across to his car. I imagined repeating what he'd said to my mum, and I could just see her eyes flashing with anger to think of him trying to bribe us to break the strike. I could almost hear what she'd say.

'You great fat toad!' I shouted at him. We started to run, fast.

'You great sloppy, slimy, slithery, slunky, smelly fat toad!'

I wonder if I hurt his feelings?

The next day the laundry was officially closed down, for modernisation. All the girls were put on standby pay with promises of jobs to return to, and Barbie received a cheque for £100 compensation. She went racing up

74

the street to Mike's house with it, much to my Mum's disgust, and the next minute they were roaring off to town on Mike's motor-bike to get some holiday brochures for their honeymoon. All the women came round to our house in their carpet slippers and housecoats, thrilled to bits with Mum, and we had a sort of breakfast party, with cups of tea on the go all the time. I had to go to the shop at the top of the street to get sliced bread for toast. Dad scarpered off to his allotment, and said he expected to find a kitchen full of eggs when he came back, with all those hens cackling.

But when he did come back, the kitchen was empty. I came back from my paper round at the same time as him, and we sat together, waiting for Mum, wondering what had happened. She came in at last, looking triumphant and happy. Her eyes were sparkling, and I suddenly realised what a terrible strain she'd been under the last few weeks. It had been a fight, keeping all the other women together, making them believe in what she thought was right. It had taken her away from us a bit, too. Now she was Mum again, laughing and tired. She kicked her shoes off into the carton by the door. Dad gave her an awkward hug.

'You did well,' was all he could say. Then, 'Would you like a cup of tea?'

She sat on the high stool, curling her toes over the bar. She held Dad's mug of tea in both hands and sipped slowly, with a far-away look in her eyes.

'I've been to see Mr West,' she said. 'He sent for me.'

'He's not given you the sack?'

'Oh no! He said ... I've got excellent qualities,' she

75

said shyly. 'He said ... he's opening up a laundrette in town, and he's asked me to run it for him.'

We both jumped up to congratulate her. Good old West, I thought.

'Will you get a lot more money?'

'Oh, I'm not taking it!' she said.

Not taking it! We couldn't believe her. 'You must be mad.'

'No, I couldn't possibly take it, now could I? Not yet, anyway.' She looked a little sad. 'I owe it to the girls to stay with them. They stayed out because I asked them to. It was us against him. I can't go over to his side now, one of the bosses. They'd hate me for it. Anyway, I've got to stay with the girls to make sure he gives them a fair deal. He's not daft, trying to get me off the premises. No chance! I'm staying put!'

But Dad was lost.

'I don't know! You women! I'll never fathom you!' And, completely forgetting that he'd already spent all day at his allotment, he heaved his wellies back on and stomped off there again.

'You've never had anything to do with old West, have you?' Mum asked me suddenly.

I pretended to be busy washing the pots up. 'Not as far as I know, Mum. Why?'

'Well, do you know what he said? He said I was bringing up my daughter to be as tough as me. He said we were very alike. Now how on earth did he know that, the silly great toad?'

But that was my secret.

6. The march of the winkles

All the time the strike was on Mike was in a terrible mood. He'd no work to go to, because there was no laundry to deliver. After his row with Barbie she refused even to speak to him. He kept having an awful dream that they'd put her fingers back on the wrong way round at the hospital. He kept going on about it all the time, and asking his mum and Kevin to find out for him. Then, to crown it all, his motor-bike packed up. After he'd kicked it a few times (being careful not to damage it) and had stormed off to town and missed the train and got wet hanging about, he banged back home in a worse mood than ever, wheeled his bike up the back steps and into the kitchen, and started to take it all to bits before his mum came home and found out. Kevin was delighted. Mike gave him a section to work on, and he meticulously took it apart and cleaned and polished it all before he put it all back together again. Except, of course, it didn't all go together again. There was definitely a piece missing. He couldn't remember what it was; but something was missing.

He looked at Mike who was frowning over some motor parts, quiet for the first time for days, and knew he didn't dare tell him. He rummaged under the table and in the pedal bin and even in the cutlery drawer, but it was nowhere to be seen. Everywhere he looked he left smudges of oil, and his ginger hair was covered in little black patches where he'd been scratching his head.

'Mike,' he said at last. 'I'm just off out for a bit.'

'Have you done it, kid?' Mike hardly looked up. 'Good lad. Here's fifty p for some pop.'

Kevin wandered off down to the beach. He just wanted to stay out of Mike's way for an hour or so – perhaps by the time he got back Mike would have found the missing part and fitted it in. It was cold on the beach, with little squalls of sand blustering against the sea wall. The tide had been out hours, but the sand was still damp. He tucked himself down by the slipway, out of the wind. Not a soul in sight. It was too miserable a day for the local kids to come down, and the wrong end of the year for the Liverpool trippers. He hated to see the ice-cream hut closed down and the open-air pool boarded up against vandals. The kiddies' paddling pool was all piled up with sand drifts, because nobody came to clean it out. The gulls' cries were desolate.

Kevin was just about to turn back home when a voice called out to him.

'Hoi! Kevin!' and he turned to see a very large man sitting in a donkey-cart, which was trundling over the sands towards him.

'Donkey-man Mooney!' shouted Kevin. He ran over to the cart and caught hold of the reins, nuzzling the brown donkey between the ears. 'Where've you been? You didn't come this summer. We missed you!'

Donkey-man Mooney grunted and heaved till he had pulled his heavy body round and swung himself to the ground. He pushed back his cap so the black coils of hair snapped up like springs. His wide, creased face collapsed into wrinkles when he smiled.

'Missed me, did you? I didn't think you'd be missing me! It's been a bad summer for me though, right enough. I lost all my fleet of donkeys Kevin love, except Rebecca here.'

Rebecca swung her head round mournfully.

'All of them?' said Kevin. 'Bingo, and Josh? And Harry Cobbler?'

'Ah, they all died, Kevin. They were all old men.'

'But what about Vi and Bathsheba? What happened to them?'

'Sure, they've retired. I couldn't afford to keep them, not when they stopped working for a living. They've gone.'

'Poor old things,' said Kevin softly. But he was thinking of Donkey-man Mooney. How did he manage without his donkeys? He'd been coming to the beach with them every summer for as long as Kevin could remember, and Kevin had often spent whole days helping him, cleaning the donkeys, feeding them, and sometimes taking the reins of one as it pulled the donkey cart.

'I bet Rebecca's lonely,' he said, and he rubbed her bristly nose. She flicked her ears casually.

'Ah well, she works hard, the little lady. We've a paper round mornings and evenings now. We keep each other company.'

Kevin looked in the donkey-cart, which was more like

a boxed-in bus-seat balanced on pram wheels than anything else. There was a strange assortment of objects
cluttered on the base; a plastic bucket, some returnable
pop bottles, a lady's rainhat, a dog lead.

'You having a jumble sale in there?'

'Them's me findings,' said Mooney proudly. 'It's
amazing what you can pick up on the beach, that careless
folks don't miss.'

'So that's what you're doing here is it, beach-
combing?'

'Well, yes and no, Kevin. We came along back for old
time's sake, but, well, it makes me sad to think of my
fleet of donkeys all lined up in their bright harnesses by

the jetty there. Didn't they love to see the children coming, Kevin? Didn't they love to set their little bells jingling and trot along the sand? Ah, but memories are no good to any man – they're worse than indigestion, the way they keep repeating on you. I'll not come back, Kevin. No, I'll not come back again.'

They walked together along the sands towards the rocks, with Rebecca and her cart snorting and creaking beside them. Mooney stood quietly and looked over the flat sands, empty of sea, and said, half to himself, 'You wouldn't like to be coming out with me for a last look at the little island, would you?'

'The march of the winkles?' said Kevin. 'Come on, Donkey-man Mooney, I'll race you there.'

So they set off on a bizarre race, as they had done many times before, across the sands to Periwinkle. Behind Kevin, the Irishman and the donkey-cart heaved and shouted and grunted as the wheels choked in the sand. Kevin ran jubilantly, his feet slapping on the wet sand, and waited, panting, at the edge of the gully that surrounded the little island: Periwinkle – a cluster of rocks, white with shells. No more than a perch for sea-gulls.

Rebecca and Mooney arrived, spattered with mud and breathless from the chase. Mooney gave the donkey an apple and then left her by the gully, and paddled across after Kevin. The boy scrambled up to a small rockpool, and Mooney clambered up as quietly as he could for a man for his size.

'Right,' he said. 'Now stop your breathing, Kevin, or you'll frighten the little things to death.'

But Kevin, who had just run over nearly two miles of soggy sand to win the race, was gasping for breath like a landed fish. He lay face downward across the rock slab, his oil-streaked hair dipping in the pool, his breath like a tornado across the water. Yet even as he lay there, and his breath quietened and the surface of the pool became smooth again, he could see a sudden movement from one of the shells in the water, then another, and over there another; a tiny twist, a gentle curl, a fraction of an inch at a time, till every winkle and limpet and snail was on the move. Mooney chuckled and pointed at the tiny movements.

'Just look at that little fellow there, spinning round. He'll be getting himself dizzy. And look at him, climbing right over that winkle. Too lazy to walk round him. He's waiting for the little fellow underneath to get up and carry him, that's a fact. Give him a poke, Kev, push the divil off!'

It was peaceful there, watching the slow, silent march of the shells, and the two lay stretched out over the prickly rock, looking down below at their reflections, and chatted about the summers they had spent together. Kevin told Donkey-man Mooney about Julie starting up at the convent school, and about the strike, and Barbie's fingers, and Mike's motor-bike, while Mooney tittered and tutted. He had known all of them so long that they were like a family to him.

Suddenly Kevin pointed out that the winkles seemed to be turning about and scurrying to the little black patches they had left in the bed of the pool.

'What are they in such a hurry for?' he said.

Mooney heaved himself up and sniffed the damp air speculatively. 'It's no wonder,' he said. 'They're claiming back their homes before the tide sweeps them away. Come on Kevin, we've talked the tide back in!'

And sure enough, when Kevin stood up on the rock he could see that the gully around the little island was filling up rapidly.

'Mooney, what shall we do? It's high tide – these rocks will soon be completely covered.'

'Come on,' shouted Donkey-man Mooney. 'We've no time to get back to the mainland – we'll have to wade across to the big island and stay over till the tide goes out again.'

Down by the gully Rebecca was braying nervously. The water was already lapping round her hooves. Mooney caught her reins and pulled her gently.

'Come on, old lady, come on,' he coaxed. 'A little paddle will do your corns good now!'

But Rebecca squared herself against the pull of the reins and rolled her eyes in fright. She held her head up and brayed as the sea-gulls wheeled above her like vultures.

'Get yourself away Kevin,' shouted Mooney. His face was purple as he pulled and heaved at Rebecca's reins, and the veins on his arms stood out like knots. Kevin looked round helplessly. He could make the big island easily, on his own. He reckoned he could make the mainland, in a hurry, with a hungry tide snapping at his heels. But how could he run off and leave Donkey-man Mooney and old Rebecca out there?

'We'll make it all right,' he said roughly. He leaned

83

against the donkey's hindquarters and pushed. She kicked out at him angrily and staggered forward as she unbalanced herself. Mooney struggled with the strappings of the donkey-cart.

'Come on, Rebecca, you'll go better without that.'

Suddenly Rebecca was charging at full speed towards Hilbre Island, with Mooney dragging behind her trying to guide her away from the gully. Water trickled towards them across the sands between the two islands, spilling over the tops of the gullies and dangerously hiding them. Sand sucked at their feet, with water bubbling through. They reached the edge of the gully separating them from the island by about twenty-five yards or more now, and looked anxiously at the brown water that creamed and curled in front of them.

'How deep would you say it is?' asked Kevin.

Mooney shook his head. The water rushed ominously past, sucking at their ankles. Rebecca reared in fright. Suddenly they heard a voice shouting from the island to them. A man was standing on its highest point, his hands cupped round his mouth, yelling to them.

'It's the warden. What's that he's saying?'

'Go back!' The voice came to them, faint on the wind. 'These currents are dangerous. Go back!'

'Glory be to God, we can't,' moaned Mooney.

'We can't!' shouted Kevin.

'Go back,' yelled the warden. *'Go back!'*

It was Rebecca who made up their minds for them. She charged towards the gully, shied, pranced sideways away from it, and turned towards the little island.

'Right, then,' said Mooney. 'Come on Kevin, we'll have to stick it out on Periwinkle.'

'But the tide ...' began Kevin. But what was there to say? Soon the tide would cover the rocks.

They stumbled after the donkey, slithering in mud that filled with foaming water with every step they took. Kevin felt the mud suck at his gym shoe and gradually close over it. He pulled his foot free. Now the slimy mud oozed between his toes, dragging him down with every step. They floundered up to the narrow gully surrounding Periwinkle like a moat and splashed into it, up to their waists in swirling water. Mooney cursed and yelled at the rigid Rebecca. She planted herself in the sinking mud at the edge of the gully.

'Get across, you hairy spider! Swim, you great lump of seaweed!' They heaved and struggled, with the water washing round them and their clothes clinging to them like dragging hands, and unbelievably, at last, Rebecca came – plunged into the gully and ploughed across to the other side; slithered and scrambled up to the top rocks of Periwinkle. Safe, at least for the moment.

Donkey-man Mooney and Kevin heaved themselves up the rocks after her. The warden on the big island was still there, waving at them. Kevin stood up and waved back, helplessly, as the rush of water swept between the two islands like fire through a forest. Mooney stood with his arms around Rebecca's neck, watching the little donkey-cart drifting and twisting and finally floating away from the island. His eyes were bright with tears.

'We should never have come back here Rebecca,' he kept saying.

Below them, the wet rocks gleamed with the slap of the waves, and the cold spray showered up to them. The little pool they had sat by filled up and overflowed, and deep in the water the limpets and winkles clung to the rocks, immovable. Kevin stood gazing out as the brown waves crept along the sands towards the mainland. Suddenly he shouted, 'Look! Over there by the slipway! They're sending the lifeboat out to us! They're coming to rescue us!'

How many times had he raced along the beach when the lifeboat alarm had gone off – bang, bang, bang – setting the dogs howling and the sea-gulls screaming?

How many times had he run alongside the boat when the tractor pulled it over the sands towards the sea, and shouted, 'Take us with you! Let me come too!'

He scarcely noticed that the water was climbing up round his ankles by the time the boat throbbed up to the rocks. He scrambled down, knee-deep, waist-deep, shoulder-deep, into the arms of his brother's best mate Pete, and was lifted onto the boat. Donkey-man Mooney and Rebecca dragged themselves down the rocks. Mooney was heaved into the boat like a floundering fish, and Rebecca, suddenly deciding that she could swim, floated to the side of the life-boat and stepped on board elegantly.

The crew laughed.

'I've done some daft things in my time,' said Pete. 'But I've never had to rescue a drowning donkey before!'

Of course, as soon as the lift-boat guns went off, Julie and I charged down and along the front to the life-boat

house. We were too late to see it being launched, so we sat on the railings chucking bread at the gulls, and waited for it to come back in. Most of the kids from school were down there, and Mike came down on his bike, purring up and down the prom like a tiger on the prowl.

'I bet he's looking for our Barbie,' said Julie. Sure enough, when Mike saw us he swung his motor-bike round and came to rest at the kerb near us.

'Has your Barbie got her bandage off yet?' he shouted at the top of his voice, over the vibrations of the motor.

Julie shook her head. I knew what was coming, because Kev had told me about Mike's bad dreams.

'I suppose . . . I mean, they did put her fingers on the right way round, didn't they?'

I thought Julie was going to fall off the railings with laughing.

There was a sudden cheer from the kids on the slipway, and we turned round to see the life-boat swinging round to head back in. The engine cut out as she approached the slipway and as she floated in we all shouted with laughter, for standing at the front, like the figurehead of a Viking ship, was Rebecca.

But I couldn't believe my eyes when I saw Kevin.

When the boat had landed and rescued and rescuers were on the slipway Rebecca stood modestly, being made a fuss of by all the kids. Donkey-man Mooney shook hands with the life-boat crew and delivered them a solemn speech of thanks.

I flung my arms round Kevin, even though I hadn't known he'd been in any danger until he'd come back safely. He hugged me as though he'd never expected to see me again, and then his eyes swung past me to Mike.

'I see you got the bike going again,' he said uneasily.

'No problem,' grinned Mike. 'I don't know what you did to her, kid, but she goes like a dream now.' He roared off down the prom, leaving Kev gazing after him.

'What's up?' I asked.

He shook his head. 'That's funny, Bee,' he said. 'When I was stuck on that island, I found a bit of Mike's motor-bike in my jeans pocket. And I thought: what if I never see our Mike again? I must get rescued; I must: or he'll never get his bike going again.'

7. Music over the mucky Mersey

It was spring, one of those mornings that doesn't know whether to burst into tears or run off with everyone's washing on the line. Mum and Dad were at work, I was off school because the heating had broken down – a rare treat. I had just started to do some baking as a surprise for Mum when the door blew open; recipe book, flour and sugar blustered round the kitchen, and in walked Kevin, followed by the strangest bundle of a person that I've ever seen.

You know how it is when you can't stop staring at someone, even though you try your hardest not to.

She had skin like a walnut, all deep holes and wrinkles, and great black yawning eyes set deep into her head. Her hair was thick and black and probably very long, though she had it coiled at the back and held in place with a big plastic comb. Where the wind had tugged it free it lay in thick wavy strands over her shoulders. She wore a shawl obviously made from a tartan blanket, and fastened at the front with a baby's nappy pin. Underneath that was a black dress with embroidered flowers in brilliant colours at the neck and cuffs and hem, which was all I could see of it. She wore thick ribbed socks, and strong walking shoes with split seams and worn-down heels.

I took in all this in a series of stolen sideways glances while I battled with the kitchen door to keep out the wind and scooped up the flour and sugar that dusted the floor. Kevin perched himself, grinning, on Mum's high stool, and the strange lady paraded round the kitchen, cocking her head from side to side and fixing her eyes on things like a jackdaw searching for territory. She clutched to her an angular parcel wrapped in newspaper, and I noticed her fingers were long and bony, not

wrinkled like her face. There was something about her that could have been younger than my mum, thirty or so, and something that could have been as old as old Mrs Wilson, just before she died.

'Who's she?' I mouthed at Kevin. She couldn't have belonged to his family, not in a million years.

'I think she's called Ann Stars,' he whispered, and the woman whipped round, black eyes snapping.

'Anastasia,' she said. Her voice reminded me of thick black treacle. 'I have honour to be in your house.' And she bowed slightly, and dangled a bony hand towards me. I didn't know whether I was supposed to kiss it or shake it, so I did neither, just stood there with a dish cloth in one hand and a bag of flour in the other. Kevin spluttered behind me.

'I see my room now,' she said to him, 'and I have bath please.'

Kevin looked at me helplessly. 'I found her on the beach,' he said. 'She was sitting on the jetty, washing her feet in the sea. When she saw me she called me over and asked me to take her to the hotel.'

'Hotel!' I said. Anastasia stood patiently, clutching her parcel, her eyes brittle like bright beads of glass. 'And you brought her here!'

'Well, there's your spare bedroom, Bee.' Kevin was beginning to blush. 'Your mum does take in lodgers, sometimes. I thought you'd be pleased.'

I gazed at them both. Kevin was right, Mum did take in lodgers, occasionally, in summer. She prided herself on her cooked breakfasts, and the same people would come year after year to watch the golf or the tennis, or just to be by our muddy sea. But we'd never had anyone like Anastasia. Ever.

'I don't think so, Kevin.' I said at last.

Kevin looked hurt. I think he'd been really pleased at the idea of doing a good turn to my mum and to his gypsy queen, or whatever she was. We both stared at her uncomfortably, hoping that she'd understand and just go away, but her black eyes fixed mine and made it impossible for me to speak. There was something a bit magical about her.

'I have bath now,' she said, and again I thought of black treacle trickling down the side of a spoon.

Well, I can't refuse her a bath, I thought. Mum needn't even know about that. I showed her into our brand-new bathroom, and just as she was going in, still clinging onto her newspaper, she said:

'After bathing I have dinner, thank you.'

Dinner!

'Kev, you've got to get me out of this,' I said angrily.

'Tell you what,' he said. 'I'll pop down to the chippie. They should still be open.'

'Have you got any money?' I asked. 'I haven't.'

We managed to turn up four p between us. We'd be lucky to get a bag of batter bits for that.

'How about beans on toast?' suggested Kevin. 'I'm good at cooking that.'

Somehow I couldn't imagine that lovely-ugly black-eyed witch tucking into beans on toast. Not exactly hotel fare.

I rummaged frantically through the pantry, and

93

eventually chucked a packet of minestrone soup at Kevin.

'Get that on,' I ordered. 'Sounds exotic anyway. And don't let it go into lumpy frogspawn, either.'

Upstairs the tank was rumbling. Anastasia's voice, low and gentle, was crooning a slow, sad song. Thank goodness we'd had an indoor w.c. put in, I thought. We couldn't expect her to go trailing half-way down the yard.

I realised then that I already knew that Anastasia was going to stay.

I carried on groping through the larder, and at last came up with what I knew would be hidden there somewhere. The tin of salmon put by for Easter. I opened the tin feverishly, cut my thumb on the edge, and tipped the whole lot into a bowl. I mixed some salad cream and vinegar and mustard, salt and pepper, and poured it over the top. Kevin screwed up his face.

'What's that?'

'I don't know,' I snapped. I didn't know what I was doing, just obeying some calm instruction in my head. 'Just you watch that the soup doesn't boil over.'

I sliced up some tomatoes, and onion and watercress, and at the last minute an apple and an orange, mixed them up and arranged them in a ring round the salmon, pouring the juices over the top. There was just the end of a Hovis left. I cut it as thin as I could, buttered it, then laid long strips of it over the top.

'They look like her fingers,' I said, 'all long and brown and skinny.'

'It looks nice,' said Kevin doubtfully. His hair was

damp from peering into the steaming soup pan. Upstairs the splashing and crooning stopped. I shoved the salmon concoction under a low grill. We heard the sound of the bath emptying itself down the pipe.

'Get that table set, quick!' I ordered. 'You'll find the cloth in that drawer.' That was the best one, that only came out at Christmas. We worked silently and swiftly, both of us tight with tension. I put out some cheese and biscuits on the breadboard. We heard her coming slowly down the stairs, her newspaper rustling. Kevin whipped the Busy Lizzy off the windowsill and put it on the table. The moment she opened the door I switched off the soup, poured it into a bowl, and swirled some top of the milk into it.

'Please sit down,' I said. I was shaking so much I could hardly carry the soup bowl across to her without spilling it. My thumb was still bleeding. 'Don't get any blood in the soup!' I kept saying, inside my head.

She sat calmly at the table, her newspaper bundle on the floor beside her, her blanket draped over the back of the chair. Her hair was loose now, thick and heavy like a dark cloak across her shoulders.

I daren't stop to watch her eat. I wobbled back to the cooker, brought out the salmon invention which was just melting nicely on the top, and dumped it on the table.

'Come on, Kev.' I said. He was out of the door before I was.

It took us twenty minutes to get all the junk out of the little bedroom and the bed made. We crept down the stairs, unwilling to go in in case she said the food was awful, yet dying to have another look at her. We couldn't hear a sound.

'Perhaps she's gone,' whispered Kev. 'Or you've poisoned her.'

'There is coffee now, yes?' came her voice. We pushed open the door. She'd eaten the lot.

'Now I sleep,' she said at last, after three cups of coffee. 'Many days have I travelled. Tomorrow I go.'

I was relieved, yet sorry to hear this. I wanted to know everything about her: where she had come from, why she looked so sad, what she kept in her parcel. She picked it up now, very gently, as if it was very fragile, and pushed back her chair.

'My room, please.'

I felt like a servant, the way she threw her orders at me, yet something about her made me want to protect her, something that was tired and strained and about to break. I think it was something to do with the look in her eyes.

I toyed with the idea of not letting on to Mum about Anastasia. There was just a chance that she would sleep all night and not get up again till Mum and Dad had gone to work. We put all the things away and I pushed the salmon tin to the bottom of the bin. I kept pacing backwards and forwards, listening for the sound of Anastasia singing or snoring or something and by the time Mum came home at last I was in such a state that I was ready to burst into tears.

'Who was that gypsy woman that came here this

afternoon?' Those were her first words. They left me gaping at her with no time to think up a lie.

'What gypsy woman, Mum?' The wide-eyed innocent look. Mum wasn't even watching.

'You know very well what gypsy woman. I've been told about her by three women already. Did she tell you your fortune, eh?'

I wished she had. It might have helped me to think up an alibi. So bit by bit Mum wheedled the story out of me. I felt like a chicken-bone being picked dry. Then she started shouting at me, and when I asked her to keep quiet in case she woke Anastasia up that made things worse. She was all for going upstairs and dragging her out of bed, but little by little I calmed her down. I tried to tell her how special Anastasia was, not like anyone else we knew.

'There's something about her Mum,' I said. 'She isn't a gypsy. She's different.'

Mum snorted. She hadn't found out about the tin of salmon yet. At least I'd kept that bit to myself.

'She's a tramp!' Mum said. 'Special! You and your fantasies! Letting all sorts of layabouts into the house, getting us talked about. You must be off your head! You'll see, she'll sneak off without paying us a penny. And she'll carry off all our valuables ... Like ... your dad's fishing tackle ...'

Mum wasn't to be appeased. We sat in the room in silence till midnight, listening out for the sound of her. At last we went off to bed, Mum muttering about us all being murdered in the night with our own carving knife if we didn't look out. I didn't sleep all night. At last it

97

was morning and I dragged myself out to do my paper round, then persuaded Kevin to come back with me to do Anastasia's breakfast.

We were just coming out of the alley-way into our street when we saw her, running off down towards the station, her tartan blanket flowing round her, her newspaper parcel clutched tightly in her arms.

'Kev! She's sneaking off!' I couldn't believe it, that Mum had been right after all. I felt like crying.

'Come on,' said Kevin. 'Let's follow her!'

Anastasia was already on the train by the time we arrived, breathless, on the platform. Kevin just had time to throw some of his paper-round money across the

TICKETS

counter – 'Two halves to Liverpool please' – and we were on. We jumped up at every station and peered down the platform to see if we could catch sight of her, and we saw her at last, so striking that everyone turned their heads to watch her, striding past the ticket collector at Hamilton Square.

For some reason we didn't dare go up to her, or let her see us following her. We dodged in and out of doorways and behind parked cars, just keeping her in sight, ducking low when she paused to ask for directions. And off she would stride again, not even noticing how people stopped to stare at her.

We suddenly realised that she was making for the ferry. We dodged along the ramp after her, hid by the ticket booth while she swung up and down the landing stage, and as soon as the gang-plank had clattered down and the mill of people waiting to cross over to Liverpool had thronged onto the ferry, we raced on.

But Anastasia was nowhere to be seen.

We raced round the boat, Kevin taking one side while I took the other; and when we met again at the part where the gang-plank had been chained up, the ferry had pulled away with a huge throbbing of the engine and screaming of gulls. The brown waters of the Mersey slapped against the side of the boat.

'We've lost her, Kev. She's given us the slip.'

We gazed mournfully back towards the landing stage, as the boat swung away from Birkenhead and out towards the familiar clocks and towers of Liverpool.

Then we heard the music. At first it was like the high-pitched keening of the gulls, but as we strained to listen

99

to it it rose and sank in the pattern of a melody, sharp and sweet above the engine's drone and the low rush of the water. People around us were straining to listen, too.

'Someone's got a tranny on. Can you hear it?'

'Eh, it's not, ye know. It's someone playing a fiddle. Look, over there, bat-eyes. Can't you see him? That old geyser's playing a fiddle,' said one of the stage-hands.

We craned round to look where he was pointing. Kevin grabbed my arm. 'It's not an old geyser! Look, it's Anastasia!'

She was standing with her tartan shawl thrown back over her shoulders, one foot slightly forward to steady herself. Her eyes were closed and her face was more peaceful than it had ever seemed yesterday. And the music she was playing was the most beautiful I'd ever heard.

'She'll have to pack it in,' said one of the stage-hands crossly. 'Tell her to quit it. She can't busk on the ferry. She must be off her rocker.'

'Tell her yerself, mate,' said the other hand. 'It's magic, that. Music over the mucky Mersey. It's better than going to Venice. It's magic.'

People began to cluster round her in a half-circle. They reminded me of gulls drawn towards a fishing boat, hungry to see what was happening. I looked round at their faces; sad old men and anxious women shoppers and people on their way to their dull offices, and they were smiling, every one of them. Nobody said a word. The stage-hand was right. It was magic.

We were coming up against the Liverpool landing-stage, the engine juddering into silence, when Anastasia drew her bow slowly across the strings and finished playing. The crowd burst into a roar of applause, as if she'd scored a goal at Anfield. She opened her eyes and looked round at them, almost in surprise, as if she'd expected to find herself alone. She didn't look happy. I've never seen anyone look so sad. Her violin case was open at her feet, and one by one the people started to come forward and put coins in it. Even from where we were standing we could tell that the coins were silver, not copper. They shuffled silently past her, not saying a word, just tossing their coins into the case, and when the gang-plank clattered down they filed off, on their way to work or to the shops, and I thought 'They're all carrying a bit of Anastasia's magic away inside them.'

She beckoned to Kevin and me to go over to her. I felt very shy, and proud. She pointed to the case with her bow.

'You bring from the ship,' she said to Kevin, and he followed her like one of the Three Wise Men bearing his royal gift.

'Why does she look so sad?' I whispered to him, and she turned her deep eyes onto me:

'I play my music in a foreign land,' was all she said.

Kevin looked at me and shrugged.

Anastasia motioned him to put the case down, then she knelt and scooped out all the coins. She held them out to me.

'Give to your mother, and for your kindness.'

I felt a huge lump rising in my throat. She knew why we had followed her. I could only shake my head but she pressed the coins into my hands. Then she placed her violin and bow gently inside the case, wrapped it up in the newspaper, and stood up. She touched us both gently on the cheek.

'I go now to your Philharmonic Hall,' she said. 'There I think they know of Anastasia Koblenski. I thank you for your care.'

We watched her in silence as she strode up the ramp and out across the busy street, till she was out of sight, and gone from our lives for ever.

I was late getting to my paper round that afternoon. I arrived at the newsagent's at the same time as the delivery van, and followed the driver into the shop. He flung down the bundle of *Liverpool Echoes* on the floor. Kevin was there already, and I think we both saw the picture at the same time. On the front page, Anastasia, unmistakably our Anastasia, smiling out at us through the clutter of words that jumped about on the page. We both snatched at the top copy, which still had the smell of printer's ink on it.

ANASTASIA KOBLENSKI, WORLD-FAMOUS VIOLINIST, DEFECTS TO THE WEST

it read, and then followed the story of how she had fled overland to seek refuge with the only European contact she had, a violinist with the Liverpool Philharmonic. 'A proud day for our country,' the article finished.

'What does it mean?' I asked Kevin.

'It means she can't call herself a Russian any more. She's left the country as a political refugee, and she'll never, ever, be able to go back there again.'

I thought of her sadness and tiredness and the magic of the music she'd played, and how tenderly she'd carried her newspaper parcel, and I was glad that I'd taken her in and fed her, not because she was famous, but because she was unhappy.

8. Marie's monkey

Marie was a funny girl. Sometimes she could be really friendly, and at other times she wouldn't have anything to do with you. She couldn't bear you to be with anyone else though – she was always trying to break people up. She hated to see Julie and me together. When I was little I used to go to Marie's house a lot, but she was much rougher than Andrew, her brother. If she got fed up with you she used to hit you over the head with a great big pot-faced doll that she'd been sent from America. It hurt. After a few of those clouts I stopped going any more, till her mother made her keep the doll in a drawer, just to be looked at. She couldn't resist it though, taking it out like a beautiful fat baby to be nursed, then swinging it up high and crashing it down on whoever happened to be nearby when she was fed up. She used to hit Andrew with it too, and their dog, before it died.

I was glad when that doll broke. It fell out of her bedroom window one night and lay with its head smashed in little pieces on the pavement, its beautiful silk and velvet dress like a crumpled rag beneath it. She thought it was my fault, because when I'd run off that day howling because she'd clouted me on the head with it, I'd told her that she'd be sorry, I'd kill her doll for her. Sorry she was, but it was nothing to do with me. Anyway, that was years ago, when I was only seven.

I never had a lot to do with her outside school after that, especially when I'd made it up with Julie, so I was very surprised when she invited me to her thirteenth birthday party. At first I thought I was the only one going, and tried to back out of it, but then I found that Kevin was going too, as he was in Andrew's class at school. I knew Marie fancied Kev. She'd sent him a Valentine's card, but for some reason everyone thought I'd sent it. As if I'd do a daft thing like that.

It wasn't what you'd call a wild party. There were only the four of us, and Marie's mum, who was mad because Marie's dad hadn't come home yet from the Liverpool v. Sheff. United match at Anfield. He was supposed to be fetching Marie's present. We munched through the birthday tea in silence, with Marie rolling her eyes at Kevin and Andrew rolling his eyes at me, but I couldn't stand Andrew anyway because his ears stuck out, and I was mad at Kevin for laughing at Marie's stupid jokes.

Out of the kitchen we were hustled and into the room to listen to records. Marie danced on her own. We could hear her mum banging and sniffing through the washing-up, muttering about football and husbands who couldn't tell the difference between a pub and the underground. I kept looking at my watch and praying for nine o'clock to come so I could get back home to my book, when there came a noise of a singing and stamping feet down the passage, the door was kicked open, and in walked Marie's dad, pink from the cold and reeking of drink and tobacco. He had his coat pulled across his chest to conceal a strange lump, and he was full of himself.

'Where is she then?' he shouted, 'where's the Birthday Girl?' although she was in the room next to him lit up with excitement. 'Right, close your eyes. I've got the best pressie you ever had!' And he undid the top button of his overcoat. Out peeped a little brown inquisitive face with eyes as bright as shiny new pennies.

'A monkey!' shrieked Marie. 'A monkey, for me!'

The monkey leapt suddenly from his warm hiding-place, shinned up the curtains, and sat on the rail, pointing down at us and chattering excitedly.

'What sort of a present do you call that?' demanded Mrs Wood, who was never satisfied with anything. 'You told me you was bringing her a new pair of skates.'

'Well, I met this sailor in a pub,' explained Mr Wood. 'And he asked me if I wanted to buy a monkey. How could I say no! Look at him love, he's beautiful. Hey, he reminds me of you!'

I could see what he meant.

Marie was over the moon with excitement, and for a time the kitchen was in a state of uproar as we clambered over chairs and the draining-board and each other trying to get the monkey down. He seemed to prefer things at ceiling level. At last it was Kevin who coaxed him down and put him gently into Marie's arms. I don't know which of them was shaking the most, Marie or the monkey. Of couse she had no time for any of us then,

so the only thing left for us to do was to thank Mrs Wood for the tea, and go off home. By this time, of course, I wanted to stay. I kept thinking of his cheeky little face and the way he clutched his arms and legs tightly round you, like a small baby.

We were a bit short on pets in our road. Kev still looked after the White Queen that he'd bought for Mrs Wilson, but she was old now, and pretty boring, even for a rabbit. The snotty-nosed twins down the road had white mice which they sometimes used to bring to school and shove into people's lockers and packed lunches. My dad kept pigeons. I loved the gentle noise they made, but they made me feel itchy – I couldn't bear to touch them. Then there were Julie's guinea-pigs, racing round the house all the time. I think the favourite pet up to now was the tortoise that someone had given to Weird George. He used to take it for walks along the prom, and I wouldn't be at all surprised if he took it to bed with him. He was terrified of it running off down to the railway lines and getting squashed by a train, so he'd painted 'I am George's toytoyse' on its back, so that anyone who found it wandering off in the wrong direction could turn it round and send it back home.

But Marie's monkey put everything else in the shade. She was famous for it. Everyone wanted to come and see it, and kids at school kept inviting her to tea, hoping she'd bring her monkey with her. She gave a talk about it at assembly, and told us all about Gibraltar, where it came from. Mr Murphy said 'And of course, when you got it, it had just come out of quarantine, hadn't it Marie?' She looked at him blankly for a minute and then said, 'No it hadn't. It had just come out of a pub, the night Liverpool lost four-nil to Sheffield United.' And we all booed and that was the end of that assembly.

One Saturday morning Marie brought her monkey over to my house. She'd bought a lead for it, and dressed it up in a little silk and velvet outfit made from the dress that belonged to the doll she used to hit me on the head with. I recognized it after all those years. It hopped after her into the kitchen and sat looking up at her with its wise little face, like a little brown old man that had shrivelled up in the rain.

'Hello, Midge!' said my mum, and Marie and I looked at each other and laughed. We had been trying to think of a name for him all week. The monkey waddled over to Mum, swung his arm round, scratched his head, then held his hand up to her. She bent down and shook it. Midge it had to be.

'I've come to see if you'll come to New Brighton with me, Bee,' said Marie. 'To the fair. I thought I'd take Midge.'

'I'll come if Julie can,' I said.

Marie still couldn't stand her because Julie had dancing lessons, and she was always showing off skating in the entry. But I knew she wouldn't go on her own.

'All right,' she said at last, crossly. 'Bring your precious Julie. And then I suppose Andrew and Kevin will want to come too. But if we get any money, it's mine.'

'What money!' said my mum sharply. 'You're not going begging are you, just because you've got a monkey dressed up in fancy clothes? You ought to be ashamed of yourself, Marie, making a fool of the poor little thing!'

109

Marie just flounced out of the kitchen, with a sharp tug at Midge's lead. Midge side-stepped after her, taking a swift rummage through the pedal bin on the way and leaving a trail of egg-shells and bacon rind behind him.

In the end we all went – Marie and Midge, Kevin and Andrew, Julie, on skates, me, and Weird George, who just trailed down the road and onto the bus after us without being asked.

There were problems from the start. Marie was sent upstairs with Midge – in fact the conductor didn't want to let her on the bus at all to begin with.

'No monkeys allowed on Crosville buses!'

'But it's only like a dog really,' she pleaded. 'Only nicer. And there's no notice to say they don't allow monkeys on!'

'Well, get upstairs with it quick!' said the conductor. 'And if the inspector gets on, shove it under the seat. I don't know, kids these days!'

Marie flounced up the stairs, and half-way up she shouted, 'Eh, Mr Conductor. See that kid with the spiky hair? He's got a tortoise in his pocket. Didn't make him go upstairs, did you?'

But the conductor ignored her. He was too busy telling Julie she couldn't travel on a Crosville bus in roller skates.

When we arrived at New Brighton the fair was in full swing. The season had just started after a disastrous winter of wellies and cold-sores, and everyone had turned out into the sunshine ready to enjoy themselves. There's something about the music and the smells of fairgrounds that always makes me feel excited. Kevin and Andrew made straight for the dodgems. They had five goes on them and only paid once. Julie and I lost all our money in the arcades, then wandered round feeling fed-up, watching the kids on those silly little grey shiny horses that go endlessly up and down, round and round, while their mums wait in a patient smiling circle round them. We saw Weird George gazing longingly at the Helter Skelter. He kept walking up to it, then wandering slowly away, till at last he made up his mind, dashed up

the stairs behind the little ones, waved majestically from the top, and careered down it. Half-way down he lost his nerve. He clutched onto the side, his face the colour of bleached sea-weed, and inched himself down, hand over hand, his eyes closed tight with terror. When at last he reached safety he sauntered casually over to where Marie was standing and leaned against the side of a candy-floss stall. After a bit he fished in his pocket and brought out his tortoise, which he placed on the ground next to Midge. Midge was delighted. He poked at it, sniffed it, tried to turn it over, and then sat on it.

'Don't you squash my toytoyse!' shouted George, miserable. Marie pretended not to know him but muttered through her teeth.

'You're not getting any of the money, if that's what you're thinking!'

'You have to do something else, besides being a monkey, if you want to get money,' I said. I was thinking of Anastasia and her beautiful music. 'Why don't you ask Julie to do some skating for you?'

You'd think I'd asked her to cut off Midge's tail, the look she gave me.

Anyway, it all seemed a bit of a failure, the whole thing. Julie and I left them to it and waded out to the fortress. You could hear the shouts and screams of the fairground from there – you could even pick out little squeaky voices shouting 'Look, a monkey! Look at that little monkey!' But we knew they'd be only stopping to have a look, not offering money, as Marie hoped.

It was hunger that brought us back, and the hope that someone had got enough money left to buy one hot dog between us. We could just pick them out through the pushing people, Marie and George looking round, bored, and Kevin and Andrew laughing their heads off on a zig-zagging helicopter roundabout, high up in the air. Suddenly I heard Marie scream.

Her voice cut through all the jangle of music and voices and shouting. I jumped up onto one of those infants' roundabouts and I saw everything that happened, though I was too far away to do anything about it. Two lads who had been hanging round Marie and chatting her up for hours suddenly made a lunge at her – that was when she screamed. I saw one of them push her back while the other one made a grab for Midge's lead, picked him up and made off through the crowds, the monkey tight in his arms.

George was shouting 'Don't you take my toytoyse' and waving his arms about as though he was trying to swim after them. The two lads dodged in and out of the pushing, curious crowd; while Marie sobbed and George shouted and Julie and I slithered our way between the prancing merry-go-round horses, all the time jumping and twisting to try to keep the thieves in sight.

Suddenly Andrew and Kevin were there, dangling dangerously from the arm of the moving helicopter ride. A woman screamed as Kevin swung his legs out and leapt to the ground just as one of the lads was racing past, flung himself at his knees in one of his famous rugby tackles, and brought the lad down. The lad crashed to the ground, let go of the lead, and instantly Midge was away, dashing like an overgrown rat through the legs of the startled onlookers. Women scattered in fear. Andrew swung himself over a roundabout barrier, skidded across the moving floor to the other side, dived headlong at the snaking lead and lay, gasping, with the quivering Midge grasped in his arms. Marie rushed over and gathered her monkey to her. He was whimpering and shivering with fright – and so was she.

We trailed off home in silence. When we got off at our stop Marie was still shaking. 'I nearly lost you, Midge,' she kept saying. 'I nearly lost you.'

'You shouldn't have taken him there in the first place,' said Julie. 'Trying to get money out of him. It isn't right. If you ask me, that monkey's more trouble than it's worth. You'd be better off without him.'

I don't think Julie said it out of spite. She's not like that. But if she'd known what was going to happen, she'd never have said that. I don't think she'll ever forgive herself for what she said.

It happened two days later. Midge seemed to have been with us for ever. I'd got into the habit of popping in to Marie's on my way back from my paper round, just to have a little play with Midge. This time, though, she was waiting for me at the street door, and I could tell she was worried when I came out of the entry.

'Come and look at Midge, Bee,' she said. 'Don't you think he looks pale?'

Well, it's difficult to tell whether a monkey is looking pale or not, but he certainly looked different. He kept pulling back his lips to show his teeth, in a weird sort of angry smile, and his eyes were burning bright. He was shivering and gibbering and every so often he would go rigid and then start leaping round the room in a fury, tearing at the cushions and the curtains and swinging on the pictures. He knocked the mirror down and it crashed into tiny pieces onto the hearth – that seemed to make him worse, causing him to roll over and over in agony, twisting himself into a tiny quivering ball and staring up at us with a frothy grin.

'Get him out! Get him out of here!' shouted Marie's mum. We none of us knew what to do. She scurried after him, helplessly straightening up the ripped cushions and the bits and pieces that he'd scattered round the room in his wild stampede.

Marie's dad was coming up the road with my dad. He must have heard the noise out in the street because he came running down the passage and into the room. He took one look at poor Midge and pushed us out of the room, slamming the door behind him.

'Have any of you touched him?' he shouted. 'Has he bitten anyone?'

We shook our heads, too frightened and worried to speak.

'Don't any of you go in there, do you hear? I'm sending for the police.'

He raced out of the house and the next minute we heard him shouting from out in the road: 'The little devil's got through the window!' We rushed outside. By this time all the neighbours were out and kids were running up from the bottom of the street and along the entries from the side streets. Midge was hanging by one arm from the top of the window, and just as someone was leaning across to grab him, he launched himself across to a drain-pipe, hunched his tight little body around it, and then scampered up it like a squirrel scurrying up a tree.

Now he had a whole terrace of rooftops to run along. He ran backwards and forwards, balancing like a high-wire walker on the spine of the roofs, perching on chimney-stacks, slithering across the tiles and dipping dangerously down to the gutters. Sometimes he would stop still and hug himself, moaning, and then he would caper off again, out of sight behind the chimneys, leaping and bobbing, staggering and hopping, swaying to steady his skidding feet.

Everyone in the street was out now, and dozens of people I'd never seen before. A bus had parked across the top of the street, and all the passengers and the driver and conductor had clambered out to see what was happening. We were all running up and down the street, following Midge's flight, uselessly holding up our arms to him and calling his name.

The police came without anyone noticing. I saw Marie's dad run up to one of the men, white with worry. I could hear people around me saying 'Rabies, rabies, he might have rabies.' Midge stopped just above Julie's house, curled himself, whimpering, below the chimney stack, and then took a slow step forward. It was as if he was giving himself up. And I saw it, I think I was the only one, I saw the policeman bring his arm up, level it straight so he was looking right along the gun, take aim, and one clean shot like a whip reached its mark. Midge flung his arms upwards, and then fell, rolled and slid over and over down the tiles to the gutter, hovered on the ledge, and then smashed to the ground.

All night I kept dreaming about it, but every time, just before he landed on the ground he changed into that American doll in its silk and velvet dress and its huge pot head smashed in pieces on the pavement.

I called to see Marie the next day, but her mum said she was too upset to see anyone yet. 'That monkey had rabies, you know. He should never have been brought here,' she said.

'He was a lovely present though, wasn't he Mrs Wood?' I said. She shrugged wearily and then went into the kitchen and brought out a brown paper parcel. Inside was a pair of second-hand roller skates.

'These were on the step this morning, addressed to Marie. Did you leave them for her,' she asked.

I shook my head. 'No, it wasn't me,' I said. 'But I've a good idea who might have sent them.'

9. On the trail of the wild one

On Monday morning the police came to our school. Marie and I were called out of class, and when we arrived at the headmaster's office Kevin and Andrew and George were there. The police wanted to question us about the two big lads at New Brighton, who'd made a grab for Marie's monkey and would have got away with him, too, if it hadn't been for Andrew and Kevin. They were concerned in case either of the monkey-snatchers had been bitten by Midge in the chase, and had caught its dreadful disease. We all looked at each other in silence. We knew it was a very serious matter. The police said they had put word over Radio Merseyside and in the *Echo*, but that we were the only ones who could really help. Kevin knew one of them, he'd told me he did, yet he said nothing. I glared at him, but he kept his head right down, and his face was flaming red. What was the matter with him? I kept thinking of poor little Midge in his silk and velvet outfit, clinging to the roof-tops before he was shot down.

'Kevin!' I hissed at last, and he twisted round in his chair, away from me, glaring out of the headmaster's windows across the yard.

'Come on Marie, you must remember something!' coaxed Mr Murphy.

Marie was close to tears. She'd had a terrible weekend. 'They were big lads,' she said at last. 'And one of them was nice-looking.' (Trust her to notice that.) 'He had blue eyes and yellow hair, and he was wearing a denim jacket with all badges on.'

'Good!' said the policeman. 'And was he the one who grabbed your monkey?'

Marie shook her head. He was the one who'd pushed her over. She'd never even noticed the other one.

Mr Murphy sighed and shrugged at the policeman. I kept my eyes on Kevin. At last I said, very pointedly, 'One of those lads was about the same height as your Mike, don't you think so, Kev?'

He twisted himself round in his chair and sort of uncurled himself from it as if his legs didn't really fit him any more. His face had gone from scarlet to white so his freckles stood out like random blobs of orange paint. 'I'd like a word with you on my own please, sir,' he mumbled.

We were all sent off to class, feeling mystified and cheated. What could Kevin have to say that we shouldn't know? Five minutes later he went off in the police car. He came back during rural studies, but avoided all eyes stubbornly. We left school together, but his frown made me keep my distance. I crossed the road just in front of him, hoping he'd catch me up, then I noticed Mike's motor-bike waiting near the paper-shop. Kev ran past me towards the figure on the bike.

'Mike! Where've you been?' he shouted. 'I've been looking all over for you!'

And then the lad on the leaning bike turned to look at him. For a second their eyes met, held each other. Then the rider turned and kicked off, down the main road and out of sight. Kev was slumped against the shop wall, gazing after the bike. I ran up to him. Two things I was sure of – first, that the motor-bike belonged to Kev's brother; second, that the lad on the bike wasn't Kev's brother. The third thing I wasn't sure of, but, as far as my memory could tell – I thought it was one of those two lads from the fairground that the police were looking for. It didn't make sense.

'Kev ...' I said. 'That lad ... wasn't he the one ...'

To my amazement he jumped up and started running off.

'Leave me alone, Bee!' he shouted. 'You've done enough, with your interference. Just leave me be!'

And I did. I've never seen him like that before.

I didn't see him again until the whole business was over and done with, and then he told us all, me and Marie and Julie and Andrew and George. We all sat on the wall outside the laundry and he told us one of the most exciting stories we'd ever heard. And it was all true.

That morning at school he'd told the policeman that when he had brought down the monkey-snatcher at New Brighton fair the lad had pinned him down to get a good look at his face and had hissed at him: 'Mike Proctor's kid brother! Right little turnip, aren't you? That's two of you in for a scalping then!'

121

Kevin had vaguely recognised him as someone Mike used to hang about with, two or three years back, and he'd told Mike about it that night.

'Biff!' Mike had said. 'Old Biff, the wild one! Out of Borstal and after my scalp.'

And then Kev had remembered. The gang Mike had knocked round with just before he left school had been caught raiding a warehouse on Birkenhead docks – and it was Mike who had given them away to the police. It had been a bad time for him – Biff, his best mate, had been sent to Borstal, and the other two had got probation. Mike had been praised by the police, but he'd felt like a real traitor. It was Barbie who had made him do it; he'd just started going out with her then and she'd made him do it to prove that he didn't intend getting into any more trouble. And he didn't; everyone in the street said how much he'd changed since he'd started going with Barbie. But he'd never forgotten the day he'd gone to the police and betrayed his friends to them. And neither, apparently, had they – Biff was back, and lusting after Mike's blood.

'I don't want to hear any more about him,' said Mike to Kevin. 'You've never heard of him, see?'

But that was before anyone had known Midge had rabies.

So when the police asked us if we could help them to trace the lads, Kevin was torn in two. He didn't want to do anything that might get Mike in trouble with Biff, or, even worse, with Barbie; but what could he do, when for all he knew Biff might be seriously in need of medical help? If Biff died, would that be his fault?

In the end he told the police that he thought his brother Mike would be able to help. He begged them to take him down to the laundry with them, hoping to explain everything to Mike before they did, and so he drove with them in the police car, not feeling a bit proud, past his house with all the nosey neighbours looking.

As they swung into the laundry-yard and climbed out of the police car Kevin was sure he saw a figure at the gates, lurching back as if to hide. He half turned, and as he did so the figure slipped out of the yard and ducked behind the wall at the other side.

'That was him, I'm sure,' said Kevin.

'Who, your brother?'

'No, Biff, the one who pinched the monkey. Didn't you see someone going out of the gates?'

But the lad was off and out of sight before the policeman had decided which direction to look in; down the side road and away, and not even the sound of his running feet left.

'Are you sure, lad?'

'No,' admitted Kevin. How could he be sure, when he'd only once seen Biff face to face, anyway?

They went into the laundry office, where Toady West eyed them with great suspicion, asking if Mike had been up to something. Kevin felt miserable. He could see girls in white turbans bobbing about in the steamy workroom, and he knew it wouldn't be long before someone whispered to Barbie that there was a policeman looking for Mike.

But Mike wasn't there. He was supposedly just about due back from the morning delivery. They waited and waited, while Toady West smirked knowingly and more and more white turbans bobbed their way towards the window. Eventually Kevin was sent back to school, and as he raced up the road, and past his house, he noticed that Mike's motor-bike was missing from the side entry.

Things were beginning to feel uncomfortable.

Not until he came out of school that night and recognised Biff on his brother's bike did Kevin know, for sure, that something had gone wrong. He didn't know what to make of it – still less did he know what to do about it. He didn't go on his paper-round, but went down to the beach where the brown tide was just edging up the slipway and knocking the little boats. He didn't know what to do with himself. If it was Biff waiting in the laundry-yard for Mike, and he'd seen Kevin with the policeman, he must have thought that Mike had got on to the police about him. So instead of waiting at the laundry to bash Mike up, he'd pinched his bike. But why had he waited outside school, deliberately, so Kevin would see him on the bike? Was it his way of telling Kevin that he'd already taken his revenge on Mike; had already scalped him? And that it was Kevin's turn next?

'I hope that monkey did bite him,' shouted Kevin to the mocking sea-gulls. 'I hope Biff does get rabies!'

He couldn't believe his eyes when he walked into their kitchen and found Mike sitting at the table, his ginger hair intact.

'Mike!' he gasped. He'd never been so pleased to see his brother before. 'I thought Biff had got you! I thought he'd scalped you!'

124

Mike laughed. 'You want to stop watching all them gangster films. Biff might be a wild one, but he's not getting any of my hair for his trophies. I think he's pinched me bike though.' He shoved his chair back angrily. 'And if he has, it's your fault.'

'He has pinched it. I saw him on it ... I thought it was you. He was waiting for me ... Then he just scarpered, on your bike! But where did you get to? This policeman came down to school and we went to West's for you ...'

Mike was off then, about interfering kid brothers and Toady West wanting to know all his business and Barbie chucking her engagement ring back at him again ... 'I've told you kid ... if it's the police ... or Biff ... I don't want to know about them. They're bad news ... they're all in the past ...' Poor old Kevin didn't get a chance to speak up for himself, because no sooner had Mike finished with him than his mum appeared, a bag of kippers in one hand for their tea, and the other hand free to clout whichever of them was nearest to her with.

'What have you been up to, the pair of you?' she shouted. 'If I'm not sick of flippin' neighbours asking me what you were doing in a police car ... and what they wanted with you, young man! Marie Wood's mother's got a nose like a vacuum cleaner, she's been in and out all day looking for bits of muck to sniff up!'

'It's a pity she didn't hoover up Biff when he was sneaking off with my bike then!' Mike's temper matched his hair – it was fierce. 'That's where I've been all afternoon – trying to find my bike. I saw it had gone when I was coming back from this morning's delivery.

I've been all over the show, looking for it. But I'm not going near the police, not this time.'

Mike reckoned that Biff had pinched his bike to bait him, and that the police would soon pick it up somewhere – abandoned, if not wrecked. And if they caught Biff on it, so much the better. But he wasn't splitting on him again. He just wanted to get Biff out of his life for good. It was Barbie he was thinking about. They were getting wed next month.

Kevin sat and brooded about that, in the kippery kitchen. He could see why Mike didn't want to have anything more to do with Biff, or the police. He'd put all that business behind him, for Barbie's sake. Biff would plague the life out of him if he thought he'd rise to the bait. But there was something else, something that was more important than Mike's reputation, or his pride, or his motor-bike, or even his wedding-day.

'Mike!' he said. 'You've got to tell the police where Biff lives! It's a matter of life and death! If he was bitten by Marie's monkey, he could die! You've got to help them to find him!'

Mike looked at him, miserable. His temper had shrivelled, like a sail that's lost the wind. 'Sorry, kid,' he said at last. 'I don't know Biff's address, and that's the truth. The police will have to do their own detective work.' And he pushed off out of the kitchen, slamming the door behind him.

It was well after midnight when he came home, though Kevin was still awake. He heard Mike coming slowly up the stairs and into his room, and saw his dark shape against the window, where he stood looking out into the street.

'Are you awake, Kev?' he asked softly. 'Listen, our kid. When I used to be in that gang – Biff's gang – we used to meet up, every month, when the moon was full. We used to meet on Bidston Hill, under the windmill. If you want to tell that to your mates down at the cop-shop, it's up to you. I'm going to bed.'

He moved away from the window, pulling the curtains sharply across. The moon hung in its full brilliance across the slate roofs of the terraces.

Kevin crept out of bed and down the stairs. He could hear his mum and dad snoring gently. He closed the back door quietly behind him, ran down the entry, across the street, and up to Weird George's house. He climbed over the wall, unbolted the shed, and wheeled out George's bike. Next door, one of Julie's little brothers cried out in his sleep. The bicycle wheels whirred like frantic wings. Kevin hoisted the bike across his shoulder, crept down the yard and up the street to the main road; then swung himself onto it and sped off along the road to Bidston. Small moths danced towards the beam of his lamp, and the wind rushed against his speed.

'There's one good thing about Weird George, apart from his tortoise,' he thought. 'He's got a smashing bike.'

It took him a good thirty minutes to cycle to Bidston, though for a long time he had the windmill in sight, silhouetted against the sky on the brow of the dark hill. He pedalled at last up the side road leading up to the observatory, and then he saw them, gleaming in the gorse-bushes at the side of the track: four motor-bikes in a row – and one of them was Mike's.

Kevin pushed George's bike deep into the bushes on the other side of the track. He ran lightly up the hill, his soft plimsolls scuffing the red dust of the path. Suddenly he stopped. He crouched behind a boulder, his whole body pounding. He could hear them, laughing. He had tracked down Biff, the wild one! The windmill gleamed white in the moonlight, with its huge sails silent and still like outstretched arms. Kevin crept slowly forward in its shadow, and clung to the back of it, welcoming the cold touch of it. If only he could leave the message without having to face up to Biff. He remembered his taunting look at the fairground, and his face outside school – cold and scornful and challenging.

He could hear the occasional suck and puff of the four lads smoking, and the scuff of their boots as they lounged on the rock below the mill. One of them said at last, 'Come on Biff, just for a laugh. Don't tell us you've gone soft after your holiday in Borstal.'

'He's chicken.'

'I'm not chicken,' said Biff angrily. 'I've told you, I don't feel up to it tonight.'

'Ah, Biff's poorly! Sympathy for Biff!' The lads were laughing at him. Kevin felt his throat clench with fear. His hands were sweating; great waves of sweat like hot blood surged across his body. He forced himself to move his feet. He pushed himself away from the shadow of the mill, and out into the full spotlight of the moon. It was as if he was stepping onto a stage.

128

The lads froze into silence. Then one of them jumped up, pushed Kevin down onto the rocks, and held him there. Biff sauntered across and stood over him. His head blotted out the moon.

'Come for your scalping, have you, turnip?'

'Who is it, Biff?'

They were all standing in a ring over Kevin now.

'Don't you recognise him? He's the kid brother of our bleating billy-goat friend, Mike Proctor. Did your Mike send you to get his motor-bike for him then? Too scared to come for it himself, was he?'

Kevin found his voice at last, shouted out so the words echoed over the hillside in the still night air. 'I've come about that monkey you pinched at the fair. It had to be shot ... it had rabies. I've come to tell you ... you might have caught it, Biff.'

Biff gazed at him, incredulous. His face was tense. One of the lads started laughing. 'Rabies! That's a good one! That's the best I've heard yet!' And one of the others joined in, and Biff looked at them both, forcing himself to smile, to laugh with them.

Then the fourth cut in. 'But I heard about that, Biff. Near the laundry. They had to shoot some kid's pet monkey because it had rabies. It's true.'

'How's your temperature, Biff?' asked one of the others, still laughing. 'How's your poor old head?'

Biff was sitting down now, hunched up against the mill, his head in his hands. The lads crowded round him, shouting and laughing. They didn't see Kevin, as he backed away from them into the shadows. They forgot all about him as he edged down the track, fumbled

in the bushes for George's bike, and rode like the wind along the silent streets to his home.

Two days later Mike heard his motor-bike roaring down the street. He'd know the sound of it anywhere. He and Kevin rushed to the door and out into the street just as Biff was getting off the bike. Mike and Biff stood looking at each other: old friends, old enemies, in silence. At last Biff held out his hand to Mike.

'I've come to wish you luck, mate, on your wedding day.' He looked awkwardly at Kev. 'And to thank your kid here, for coming out the other night. Put the wind up me all right, you did . That's where I've been till now – in Birkenhead General. Kept me in for tests – or you'd have had your bike back before now. Treated me like royalty, they did, at the hospital.'

'But are you all right ... I mean ... did you have ...' began Kevin. It sounded daft now, in broad daylight.

Biff roared with laughter. 'Right as rain!' he said, 'except for some red blobs. Know what I've got? Caught it off me kid brother ... I've got flippin' german measles!'

10. Sea-gulls and wedding bells

The first of May was a Saturday, and the perfect day
we'd all been hoping for for Barbie and Mike's wedding.
They were married at eleven o'clock at the little church
down by the sand-hills. While the bride and groom and
all their relations were at the church the rest of us busied
ourselves with preparing the street for the celebrations.
By the time the wedding cars started returning, the
whole street was in a fever of excitement – for the wedding party was to take place out in the open air, so that
the neighbours and friends of both families could join in.
It was the first street party any of us kids had been to.

The street was ablaze with colour; dancing rags and
flags were threaded across from window to window, and
looped from lamp post to telegraph pole. Long trestle
tables had been laid from end to end – from the shop at
the top of the street down to the laundry – and the
women came from their houses carefully handling iron-
hot sheets to lay across them. My mum, who had done
all the organising, was there with sheets of paper, cross-
ing off lists; and Marie's mum, who hated her for it, was
sending small children scurrying with things to do. Mrs
132

Marriot, who had made the cake and most other things, was running in and out of her hot, sweet, floury bakery of a kitchen, smiling her wet smile and bearing wooden trays with striped cloths over the top. Mr Marriot stood guard, waving his stick at the sniffing dogs and the damp-nosed twins who lusted near the meat pies. All the dads were making themselves useful, heaving chairs and stools out of their front rooms, joking about having to test the beer soon – 'We'll have to make sure it's settled, love.' Kevin was there, devastating in his first-ever suit, chasing bits of confetti from his pockets and out of his hair. His Uncle Billy was there, tuning up his fiddle for the dancing. Weird George was there, kissing all us girls for once in his life, holding out his lobster hand for all the men to shake. Julie, like a princess in her long blush-pink dress, sat as prim as a parrot so as not to disturb her new hair-do; and Marie, tight in the bridesmaid's dress she had worn to her cousin's wedding last summer, watched herself in the window. There were mums and dads and neighbours who had never talked and little old ladies and squealing babies all pushed into the sunlight together; and the only two people in the whole street who were missing were the bride and groom, Barbie and Mike.

'You're quite sure they did get married, I suppose,' snapped Marie's mum. 'I wouldn't put it past that stuck-up little madam to have changed her mind again.'

'Of course they got married,' snapped my mum in reply. She never spoke to Marie's mum if she could help it, and rarely resisted giving snarl for snarl when she did. 'I was there. *I* was invited to the service.'

'Everything's ready!' sang out Mrs Marriot, her face as pink and shiny as her gums with all the exertion.

Like filings to a magnet every child in the street streaked towards the food.

Like foghorns on the Mersey every woman in the street boomed out, 'No you don't!' and slapped at the snatching hands. 'Just you wait till the bride and groom arrive.'

'Where the devil can they have got to?' muttered Julie's mum. 'They set off here from the church an hour ago. They could have walked it here and back three times by now.'

'Perhaps the car got a puncture,' I suggested. But Julie shook her head. 'No, we'd have passed it on our way here. Perhaps the best man forgot to pay the priest, and they went back to do it.'

'I did pay him!' shouted out Pete, the best man, from behind his shiny red and pearl piano accordion. 'In fact your Mike and Barbie still owe me for that. They're probably running away from all their debts.'

'Let's have a bet on why they're late,' said Kevin, anxious to keep up the non-existent party spirits. 'Everyone write down why they think they're late, and the one who's right wins a ...'

'Piece of wedding cake?'

No-one took him up on that idea.

The twins, Eddy and Leslie, posted themselves at the top of the road as look-out guards. 'They're here! They're here!' they shouted at the approach of every black car, and after a bit we all stopped taking any notice of them at all.

The morning dragged on. The jellies bulged. The sandwiches curled. The flags sagged. Old Mrs Brown grumbled back into her house, saying she'd got a nice kipper she could have for her dinner, and that we could give her a shout if anything interesting happened. Julie's mum and Kev's mum started scowling at each other.

'Your Mike never was exactly reliable,' said Julie's mum.

'It's your Barbara that's unreliable. How many times has that girl changed her mind? Every time the tide comes in! I'll bet she's given him back the wedding ring already!' They glowered at each other, arms akimbo, over the tray of fairy cakes. The other guests stood round helplessly.

A sudden jingling of a bicycle bell robbed the mums of any further baiting, for out wobbled Weird George on his blue bike, beaming at us all as if he was one of King Arthur's bold knights.

'Don't worry everyone!' he shouted. 'I'll find them for you!' And off he wobbled, ringing his bell and shouting 'Barbie! Mike! Where are you?' We all gazed after him in amazement – the only one of us, it seemed, who had any sense at all.

'Well, I don't know,' said Julie's mum. 'And where does he think he's going to put them when he finds them? In his saddle bag?'

When they left the church, in a shower of confetti, and were snuggled up together in the back of the hired car on their way to the street party, Barbie suddenly said to Mike, 'Guess who we forgot to invite to the wedding?'

135

'Oh no!' groaned Mike. 'Not another one of your relations. Which warren does this one live in?'

'It's not a relative, Mike. It's Donkey-man Mooney! How can we get married without asking Donkey-man Mooney along?'

Mike put his arm round her. 'Because if we asked that old scalleywag along he'd have half the beer barrels emptied before we'd even cut the cake!'

'Oh, Mike.'

'And then there's that old porter you're always chatting up at the station, and Fish May stinking of wet plaice ... You'd have everyone along, you would.'

'Oh please, Mike! Just Donkey-man Mooney! After all, he is doing your delivery job for you while we're on our honeymoon.'

She had her way, of course. Several minutes later their hired car drew up outside the nettle-field in which Donkey-man Mooney's caravan was parked. Mooney was outside, painting the last touches to Rebecca's smart new black and gold cart – '*WEST'S WHITES ARE BEST WHITES*' – in a flourish of gold, across the back.

'What's this?' asked Mike. 'You're only doing my laundry delivery for two weeks, you know.'

'I'm a professional,' said Mooney, proudly. 'Besides which, and knowing your taste for changing jobs, Michael, I'm thinking it'll not be long before I'm on the permanent staff at the laundry. No offence meant, no offence at all. But just look at you both,' he added, eyeing Mike's grey suit and Barbie's long white wedding gown. 'There was no need for you to get dressed up like that just to come visiting me. Or is that your nightie you're wearing, Barbie?'

'Come on, Donkey-man Mooney! I'm too old to be teased by you any more. I'm a married woman now! We've come to invite you along to our wedding party – will you come, and will you bring your tin whistle along for the dancing?'

Mooney grumbled about his old stained clothes, and confessed that he couldn't remember when he's last had a bath, which didn't surprise either of them. The driver of the hired car sighed, thinking of the football match he'd be missing if they didn't make up their minds soon, and peeped his horn very gently.

'Your sandwiches'll be getting cold,' he muttered, just loud enough for them to hear.

'Right, I'll come!' said Mooney. 'But on one condition. You send that contraption of a car back to its garage, and let Rebecca here pull you, Barbie, like a little princess, in her new carriage.'

Mike sent off the hired car, and lifted Barbie up into Rebecca's smart new carriage. Only he and Mooney saw the streak of gold paint that smeared along the hem of her wedding dress as her skirt wiped across the new lettering.

'Not to worry,' whispered Mooney. 'She'll not be wearing this dress very often.'

Mike swung himself up beside Barbie, being careful to avoid the wet paint himself, and Mooney clicked gently to Rebecca, and off they set.

It was a long way, but who was worrying on a bright blue May morning when sea-gull cries were mingled with wedding-bells? They came down along the golf-course and onto the hard sand, enjoying the stir of excitement they caused along the beach. Small children with sandy knees and ice-cream mouths left fathers and dogs half-buried under wet sand to joint in the parade. They danced alongside the old Irishman, who was prac-tising jigs on his tin whistle, and the brown donkey, with her harnesses creaking and her little bells jangling. Proud in the black and gold donkey-cart sat the bride and groom. Barbie was radiant. She lifted back her veils and arranged her long full skirts around herself and, like Queen Elizabeth the Second, waved to the people.

It was then that Rebecca took matters into her own hooves.

With a sudden joy for life she remembered Periwinkle Island. Snorting with triumph she tossed back her head, kicked up her legs and charged at full speed across the sands. Donkey-man Mooney hollered with rage, and the reins slipped from his grasp. The dancing children cheered. Barbie screamed, clung to Mike; he stood up and roared at Rebecca, who flattened back her ears, dug her hooves in ... and cart, groom, bride and yards and yards of white wedding dress tumbled into the mud of the Dee estuary.

As Barbie sat in the waiting-room of the Cottage Hos-pital, waiting for Mike to have his sprained ankle at-tended to, she mused on the fact that it hadn't really been very long since she had sat there with two fingers hanging off, crying over a broken engagement ring. If she hadn't had that accident at work, and the compensation money from Toady West, she and Mike would never have been able to afford to go away on a honeymoon. And if they hadn't been going away on honeymoon, Donkey-man Mooney would never have been given a donkey-cart to take over Mike's job for him. And if he hadn't been given a new donkey-cart ... she turned to Mooney, who was fussing and grumbling away at her side. 'Don't worry,' she said. 'It wasn't your fault at all ...'

Meanwhile, when brave George wobbled away from our street on the first stage of his quest for the missing bride and groom, he made for the little church by the sandhills, to see if they were still there. It was the first time he had ever been in a church. He bumped his bike up the steps, pushed open the door, and peered on. No-one. Sunshine fell through the stained-glass windows and across the polished benches like jewels of light. George walked slowly down the aisle; his knees clicking, his bicycle chain ticking, his heart pounding.

Father McEvoy popped his head round the door of the vestry, and sighed. Four weddings in one day, and not even time to finish his cup of coffee in between.

'Yes?' he said helpfully.

'I'm looking for the bride and groom,' said Weird George. 'It's their wedding day.'

'I see. Well, you're a bit early, I'm afraid,' said the priest. 'They'll be about half an hour yet.'

'Oh.' Weird George's eyes flickered round the church – the statues, the flowers, the lovely lights and colours of the windows. He liked it.

'I'll wait, then.' He propped his bike against the end of a pew.

'Ah,' said Father McEvoy, thinking of his cup of coffee growing a wrinkle of skin. 'But you must take your bicycle outside, young man.'

George was horrified. 'Oh no,' he said firmly. 'It'll get nicked. I'm not leaving my bike outside no church.'

'I'll tell you what, then. We'll wheel it into the vestry and I shall keep an eye on it for you. How's that?' George watched anxiously as the priest whirred his bike from sight. He supposed it would be all right. He hovered near the vestry door.

'Well, you go and sit down, then,' said Father McEvoy, gently lifting the skin off his coffee with his spoon handle. 'Whose side are you on?'

'Side?' repeated George, mystified.

'Whose side? Are you on the bride's side or the groom's side?'

'Why, are they having a fight?'

Father McEvoy looked at Weird George in amazement. He wasn't joking.

'Oh, I see what you mean!' laughed George suddenly, and looked round, startled, as his voice woke up the echoes. 'I'm on the same side as the bride. As a matter of fact, she lives next door.'

Wearily, the priest indicated which side of the church George should sit on.

He waited. And waited.

Gradually the church began to fill up with people assembling for the next wedding of the day. Women in smart hats, men in suits, children combed and polished.

They talked together in low whispers, and slowly filled up the benches. George smiled round at them. Suddenly the organ boomed out, the people stood, and the bride in a white rustle of satin swept slowly down the aisle and came to rest at the altar rails, leaning slightly on the tall man at her side. Father McEvoy walked slowly down the altar steps. His eyes flickered past the bride, the trembling bridesmaids, the pale groom and the best man clustered before him, to the boy who had run up to join them and who was now signalling to him fiercely.

'Hey mister,' whispered Weird George. 'Can I have me bike back? This is the wrong bride and groom!'

So it was that Weird George, wobbling disconsolately down Market Street, and Rebecca, nosing her way out of the grounds of the Cottage Hospital, narrowly missed a collision. George stood there in the Saturday morning traffic, balancing his bike in one hand and holding on to Rebecca's reins with the other, not knowing what on earth to do with himself. He wandered off with them till he found a policeman on traffic duty.

'What's this?' asked Constable Harvey. 'A travelling show?'

'Please help me!' said George. He was beginning to feel tired and hungry and a bit of a failure. 'I've lost Barbie and Mike and the party's going to be spoilt and I've found this donkey and ...'

'It's not really your day, is it lad?' said Constable Harvey. 'But I happen to know who this donkey belongs to, and I wouldn't be at all surprised if that isn't him,

steaming over the horizon there, and with your lost property in tow as well.'

He was right. Along came Mooney, snorting and shouting, supporting a hobbling Mike, and beside him Barbie, the bedraggled bride, her cheeks hot with being looked at so often. With a sigh of relief bride and groom heaved themselves up into the donkey-cart, and Mooney produced two lumps of sugar; one for Rebecca, for not wandering off too far this time, and one for Weird George, for finding her.

Constable Harvey, who had known Barbie's dad for

years, for various reasons, gave her a wedding day kiss. He slapped Rebecca on her way.

'You're a wonderful advertisement for West's Whites,' he shouted after the swaying donkey-cart. 'I've never seen a muckier wedding-dress in my life!'

And they were home at last.

Weird George rode in front of them down the street, jingling his bicycle bell and shouting 'I've found them! I've found them!' and brought us all running from our houses. He was given a hero's welcome. So was Mike, whose bandaged ankle was put on permanent display for the rest of the afternoon. Barbie was rushed off for a wash and a change – how the women grieved over her wedding-dress! – and we all rushed round the tables whisking the striped tea-towels off the trays of food and plumping up the sandwiches. The buntings blazed again. Kevin's Uncle Billy started up a jig, and Pete the best man joined in with his bright squeeze-box, and Donkey-man Mooney, with only two pints of beer inside him, piped away on his tin whistle like a lark, turning and wheeling his tune to the skies. Mr Marriot, who had never done anything but shout at us kids for as long as we could remember, passed his walking-stick down to Mike and clattered out a percussion on a pair of spoons, while Mrs Marriot beamed, toothless and contented, beside him. The cake was cut, the trifles were eaten, the toasts were drunk, the twins were sick, and the old ladies nodded off to sleep. The tables were pushed back and the entire street gave itself up to dancing.

I was suddenly aware of Kevin standing beside me.

143

'Come on down to the railway bridge with me, Bee,' he said.

I followed him down the street, threading through the dancers and chairs and leaping dogs. We went down the cinder path and up onto the railways bridge. We could still hear the music from there, though it seemed like an echo a thousand miles away. Below us was the laundry yard, with Mike's delivery van parked at the side, and Rebecca's cart, ready for Monday. Beyond that; our street, pale with houses, in a light which would scarcely fade on that May night. We could see the trees and gardens of the posh houses across the main road from our street, and beyond that, but only just – the sea. Far, far out on the horizon were tiny little ferry-boats, like roofs with smoking chimneys on them. In the distance a train trundled gently. Above us, swifts, black against the sky, were screaming; and sea-gulls sobbed.

'Just think,' I said softly. 'In just over an hour your Mike and Barbie will be catching the train from here. And then they'll be off on one of those little black blobs on the sea, going across to Ireland. And when they come back, they won't belong to our street any more.'

We watched the warm light settling over the roofs of our houses.

'I know,' said Kev. 'I feel sorry for them. I'd rather live in our street than anywhere else in the world. Wouldn't you?'